The Youngest-in-Charge

by Andrew Raymere Hansley

The Youngest-in-Charge

By Andrew Raymere Hansley

Cover Designed by LeRoy Grayson

Cover Created by Jazzy Kitty Publications

Cover Pictures: Andrew Hansley and Vandick Robinson

Logo Designs by Andre M. Saunders/Jess Zimmerman

Editor: Anelda L. Attaway

Co-Editor: Andrew Raymere Hansley

© 2020 Andrew Raymere Hansley

ISBN 978-1-954425-06-4

Library of Congress Control Number: 2020925848

ACKNOWLEDGMENTS

I'm living off of experience and experiences has always been my best teacher. So please allow me the opportunity to give thanks to all the people who helped to shape my reality and experiences.

First my brothers Andre, Don-Don, and Donjuan: Right, wrong or indifferent, I would go to war with these intelligent brothers any day. I love y'all to pieces.

To my sister Tinks: You are not just the youngest, but the only girl as well. You have four brothers who's overprotective of you. You are the special one, Tinks and I love you to death.

To my kids Angie, Shaquille, Skeez, Kyri, and Andrew: God gives everyone a gift, find yours and tap into it, then shine like the stars y'all are.

To my ex-wife, Mrs. Cereza Hansley whom has given me a thousand chances. I'm sorry that I was unable to love you the way that you needed to be love—you deserve nothing less than the best, and I pray that you will one day find a husband that will appreciate your energy and love you the way that you need to be loved.

To Marvella Davis: God gave us a rose that sprouted through concrete—because I allowed the streets to swallow me whole. I was unable to be the father that I needed to be. Please except my apologies. There's not one book that teaches one how to raise a child, but if there was you could be the author. Thank you.

Crystal, we were kids and I was already in the life. Every day we wake up to opportunities, chances, and choices. A lot of my choices were bad ones, in which I had to live with the consequences. Great turnaround Crystal, you look good and doing well. Keep up the good work.

Leena, me chasing the latest gun, Jordans, and gold chains took me away from your love. You watch me leave in cuffs and didn't return until

10 years later. While away, you asked for my blessing on a situation and I respect you for that. Continue to live your best life.

Sakinah, many believe that I need more than you have to offer. What they don't know is that you are a good person and will give me the shirt off your back. See, I don't need a housewife, just someone who understands me. You are a professional hair stylist; get that money and stop playing with the process. Baby girl, I need for you to strive for better, and let the love I have for you help you along the way…

I've learned so much from each and everyone of these females; and for that I will have a place in my heart for each and every one of them.

My publisher, Anelda L. Attaway known as "Jazzy Kitty" and her staff at Jazzy Kitty Publications.

Big Shot Out to my South Bridge family, I love all you niggas!

My second home 2-6, thanks for loving me.

Riverside…

Eastside…

Westside…

Put the guns away and let's get some money!

DEDICATIONS

This book is dedicated to three women that are the CENTER of my life. They both mean the world to me: My grandmother Ms. Nina Cornish, Mrs. Lotti Gordon, and my beautiful mother Julianna Hansley.

TABLE OF CONTENTS

TABLE OF CONTENTS

INTRODUCTION

The Youngest-in-Charge is a story that includes loyalty, trust, and value vs. murder, money, and sex-with lust, envy, and betrayal on the sidelines. Who wins in these mean streets that millions call the game. It's a million ways to get money and selling drugs is just one of them.

Young Conartist, Trickbaby, Knock-out, and George Washington have a mean hustle game but will the brothers from another mother live to see 18-coming out of the grimmest projects in the city of Wilmington in the state of Delaware-where the life expectancy is 18.

The Youngest-in-Charge street movie is a page-turning manuscript that will take you on a journey that's filled with conning, scheming, and everything else that will get you killed. In fact, it's so real you will think you're at the movies.

CHAPTER 1

Spring of 2004

Conartist, Trickbaby, Knock-out, and George Washington are sitting in a stolen 5.0 Mustang in the middle of the "Southbridge Projects" that's located dead center of Wilmington, Delaware. The city "Newsweek" labeled "Murder Town USA." All four Youngest-in-Charge members got their game faces and hard hats on. There's NO time for jokes their focus is at an all-time high; when a gameplay is written up, like a pit-bull chasing a cat they're trained to go. Once young George put the Mustang in drive, each one of their hearts started dancing to its own beat. Because everyone knew their position, not a single word needed to be said when the I's are dotted, and the T's are crossed ain't nothing to be talked about. As young George whipped the Mustang down I-95 towards their destination, young Con, who is riding shotgun, reaches into his Nike bag and hands young Trick and young KO their uniforms. Twenty minutes later, they were pulling into one of the biggest malls on the east coast, "Christiana." As young George circled the mall, like a lion watching its prey, the four hungry hustlers observed every detail through the smoked tinted windows.

As young George parked the car in perfect view of the entrance, young Con goes into his pocket that's under his uniform and pulls out a stopwatch. Once the security van pulled in front of the entrance to make its rounds, young Con pushed go on the watch. Like clockwork, the van was back in seven minutes. Again, as the vans pull off, young Con pushes go.

Seven minutes later, as the van pulls up, everyone looks at each other, knowing what the other is thinking, *"If you fail to plan, you plan to fail."* Again, the van pulls off, but this time young George whips the Mustang in front of the entrance. As young KO yells, "Death B-4 Dishonor, play on playa!"

Con, Trick, and KO hopped out of the car and swiftly moved towards the entrance. To the outside looking in, it appears to be three women entering the mall. Once young George saw his Crew enter, he moved the car 25-feet forward and stopped in front of a door that read *"EXIT."* Dressed as women, the three thoroughbreds crossed the malls threshold and then the play went into action.

Knock-out made a left, but Conartist and Trickbaby kept straight. Fifteen seconds later, young Con and Trick were crossing the plain to "Zale's Jewelry Store." Con went straight to the Rolex display and Trick to the diamond rings. Before the two female employees could ask if the women needed any help, the sledgehammers were slamming through the glass, causing one of the female employees to shit on herself. While the others were stuck in a state of shock as they witnessed what appeared to be two Black women filling their bags with jewelry. Like a running back going in for a touchdown, young Trick took off running while tapping young Con in the process to let him know that they were out. Both of them ran towards the fire exit hallway where young KO was at keeping the get-a-way lane clear. After young George saw his Road Dogs come out of the exit door, he started doing the money dance after the squad jumped in the car and were on the highway.

Young KO yelled, "Get rich or die trying Mothafucka! Youngest-in-Charge Bitches! Now Con put that Lox Shit on." After young Con hit the button on the car's sound system, the lyrics came to life.

"If you love the money, then prepare to die for it. Niggas done started something."

Back at the projects, the four hustlers are seated at the kitchen table inside their Band-O, which they call the Lab. This is where it goes down; nothing is off-limits. In the kitchen is a table, four chairs, a microwave, and an icebox that only consists of Corona's, Henny, and snacks. The living room has a 52-inch flat-screen that's mounted on the wall and attached to it is a PlayStation and surround sound speakers. In the middle of the floor sits a craps table and along the wall a-sectional. It's a small table in the corner that sits a glass bowl that's filled with condoms and peppermints. Upstairs is a bathroom that's completed with a women's touch. A small closet that stays stocked and two bedrooms that's furnished with queen size bedroom sets.

The kitchen table is full of Rolexes and diamond-studded pinky rings. Thirty Rolexes and 20 rings, to be exact.

"Mario should be pulling up any minute," said young Con whose sitting at the table with one of the watches in his hand.

Mario is a young Italian boy who owns a jewelry store on South Street in Philadelphia. One day while Con was in his store plotting his next come up, Mario was in the back watching the cameras. Mario being from the streets himself he saw something special in the young Con.

"Hello, can I help you, Sir?" Mario asked.

Con, who was wearing a pair of red Tommy Hilfiger shorts, a red and white Tommy Hilfiger T-shirt, and a crisp white pair of Stan Smiths Adidas, said, "Sure, in fact, we may be able to help each other."

Then he pulled out three Rolexes of his own, two of which were identical to the one that Mario had on his wrist; from there, a fence was born, and a bond was built.

Young Con had an old soul and was before his time. His motto was, *"I ain't talking fast, you just listening slow."*

"Young George, open the door for Mario; he's pulling up now," said Con, who was still looking at the Big Face presidential.

"Con what you keep looking at that pretty motha fucka for; everything must go Nigga," said Trick, who was smiling because he knows his man wants to keep it.

The rule is no one is allowed to keep anything that's traceable back to any of the Youngest-in-Charge members. Because of the lives they lived, they needed receipts. Before Mario could knock, George swung the door open.

"What it do?" George asked, smiling.

"You the man," replied Mario while coming through the door with two of his bodyguards.

Because this wasn't Mario's first time coming to the Southbridge Projects to do business, he was comfortable with the setting. Mario also knew that the Youngest-in-Charge members were well respected in their projects and fucking with their "chicken" would leave you eating with the sharks.

"Marioooo, what's up Baby?" asked young Con while giving Mario a gentlemen's hug.

"Goodfellas, Goodfellas, how's my family of youngins?" Mario asked, "you guys met my bodyguards?"

"We have," said young Trick.

"Ok, well, let's get down to business," said Mario.

When business is in the process, only one member out of the crew does the talking; everyone else falls back until it's their turn to drive. Early in the week, Mario sent Con pictures of what to grab, where to grab it, and how much he would give for the grab.

"It's all there Mario," said Con, "the Explorers, Sky Dwellers, and Big Faces and of course your favorite the Diamond Crusted Pinkie rings.

"I love this kid; from the first time I laid my eyes on you, I knew you were a winner," said Mario while bagging up the jewelry, "what's my tag?"

"One hundred grand, but you also got to send "Santa Clause" an open gift card of his choice from your store," replied young Con.

"Done deal. Well, let's go get the chicken as you guys call it," said Mario while laughing his ass off.

The stretch cocaine white Hummer was parked out in front of the Lab and the goons that sat inside had guns that were bigger than Lil' Bow Wow. As the men approached the Hummer, the window slip down, and out came a hand with a bag that consisted of 110 grand.

"Young Con, there's an extra 10 grand in the bag," said Mario.

"What's that for?" asked young Con.

"Because I'm glad to be on you guys' team and not playing against you."

Everyone just smiled...

CHAPTER 2

The Four Hood Niggas

The four hood niggas were each other's day ones and bred out of the same poverty-stricken projects. They played in the same sandboxes, ate the same government cheese, and even broke a one-dollar food stamp down four ways. When one was seen, the others weren't too far behind. To them, everything was a hustle; they collected cans, pumped gas, carried groceries, and even sold their free lunches; and it was all for the love of a gamble. The neighborhood drug dealers loved them to the core, but to "Santa Clause," they were his kids.

Richard "George Washington" Cornish mom Kim was just 15-years-old when he was born. His dad Richard Sr. died fighting the White man's war when Lil' Rich was just three years old, which left Kim a single parent. Kim was tall, dark, and beautiful. She was blessed with big titties, a small waist, and long silky hair. Kim was arguably the prettiest in the projects, young or old. She took pride in taken care of her son. That pretty face and good pussy got her a job at Bank of America. Marvin, the executive of the bank, saw Kim shopping for her son one day and couldn't resist her beauty. Marvin lived a professional life and had a wife and two kids. But after letting the lame eat her pussy like the fat White man in the movie Harlem Nights. Marvin wanted to call his wife and tell her that he was never coming home. Marvin didn't move Kim out of the projects, but he did furnish her house and bought her a 745BMW. Kim was into young boys, but because Marvin was an asset, she knew that cutting him off would be a fool's move. So, she kept him in her pocket and fed him the pussy from a long spoon. And because the bank job was good to Kim, she figures as long as her son was straight, she was straight; and anything extra was just icing on the cake. When Lil' Rich was just a baby boy, his first full sentence was, *"Let me have a dollar."* Three times a day, he would ask his mom for a dollar, which he would get it. In his small world, everything revolved around a dollar. It was something about that White man's picture that's on the front of a dollar bill that had Lil' Rich fucked-up in the head. Kim knew her son had it bad when one day Lil' Rich asked for a dollar, but instead of handing him a dollar, she handed him a 10, but he wouldn't take it. Instead, he threw a temper tantrum until she put the 10-dollar bill back in her handbag and gave him a dollar. It wasn't until this same act happened in the projects that Santa Clause would give him the handle "George Washington."

Just a few years later, the taste of dollar bills became shitty; so, they started feeding him 50s, but the name George stayed the same. Young George was slim, tall, and dark like Kim. He had the whitest teeth, and his glow looked as if he just came home from prison. He always looked to be in deep thought, as if he were playing chess. Young George kept a mean poker face. Besides Kim, his day ones and Santa Clause was all that mattered; he kept his circle tight. George didn't even respect money. He blew it too fast and received it even faster. In his world, it was loyalty over everything.

Andrew "Conartist" Robinson was the definition of hoodlum, his mother Joy was a ghetto superstar, and it was in front of her house that you could get any drug you needed. *"Twenty-four hours a day, coke, dope, or weed-what you need,"* is all you heard on this block. The hustlers bust traps and shot dice from sunup to sundown in front of Andrew's house. Hustlers hustled until their muscles were dead sore. Nights when Joy thought her only son was in the bedroom asleep, he would be in his bedroom window watching the realest movie he has ever seen. But only this shit wasn't acting; it was the real deal. Night-in and night-out, he witnessed hand-to-hand drug sales, guns being stashed, and junkies getting knocked out for trying to be slick. It wouldn't be until "Santa Clause" would notice him in the window, toss him a few dollars, drop a jewel on him, then tell his little ass to go to bed. Then and only then is when Andrew would go to sleep.

"Jaws," who was Andrew's dad, was a con artist who took his hustle to Vegas. In a high-stakes crap game, he got caught switching the dice and was shot in the head while the dice was still in his hands. Jaws mother, Mrs. Piggy lived in the "Riverside" Projects, which was one of the deadliest sections in Delaware. Mrs. Piggy ran three gambling houses and the one that she oversaw was in Riverside. Because Andrew reminded Mrs. Piggy so much of her son Jaws, she catered to his every need. Andrew could do no wrong in her eyes. The weekends were when her gambling houses did numbers and also when she sent for Andrew. Andrew loved staying the weekends with his grandmom; to him, it was like going to hustling school. He just hated the fact of leaving his boys behind. It would pay off because he would one day teach them everything he learned.

Friday and Saturday nights would be the busiest. The crap game would be going on in the kitchen, a Tunk game in the living room, Pitty-Pat in the dining room, and Spades in an upstairs bedroom. The small project would be filled with all kinds of people; dope boys, pimps, con artists, thieves, stick-up kids, prostitutes, slowpoke brains; you name it, they were at the tables. Mrs. Piggy would cut every game and her grandson would be her partner, and the only one she trusted. He was also the store runner; he ran for cigarettes, soda, liquor, condoms, you name it, and for a small fee, he came back with it. Andrew would move from table to table, hustling with the craps being his favorite. Andrew listened to all the slick talk and manipulation being run around the table. He watched everyone's hands and movements; he was picking up what everyone was putting down. They loved him. One night while at the packed craps table, old-head Quinny was tipsy and talking shit. Andrew was waiting for this moment because Quinny would run him but never paid like he weighed.

Overall, the noise Quinny yelled, "Andrew, where you at Lil' Nigga!"

"What up Old School," Andrew quickly replied back.

"Y'all hear this Lil' Mothafucka," said Quinny handing him a 20-dollar bill and placing his order; in one swift move, the bait and switch was done.

"Why you lookin' at me like that Lil' Nigga?" Quinny asked, being loud and grabbing everyone's attention.

"Because you didn't give me enough money, you only gave me a dollar," said Andrew while holding a dollar in his hand.

Quinny was stuck and looked at Andrew in a state of confusion. He was tipsy and wasn't sure if he gave him a 20 or a dollar.

"Man, this Little Mothafucka is a con artist just like his dad," said Quinny, still not believing he just got played. Santa Clause who was on the dice, peeped the move, loved the play, then threw Andrew a 10-dollar bill; he would ever be labeled as a con artist. Young Con had the gift of gab, he would grow to talk turtles out shells, girls out of their panties, and lames out of their wallets. Young Con was a pretty-boy that stood 5'10, and he had a caramel complexion and curly hair. His game was so tight he would have you to believe that he was a Cherokee Indian, knowing Joy had nigga hair.

CHAPTER 3

Introducing Trickbaby

Calvin "Trickbaby" Johnson lived next door to young George. As a kid, Calvin wondered why so many different men would run in and out of his house late at night. This time of hour he wasn't allowed to come downstairs or his mom Shaneequa would bust his ass. One night while using the bathroom he overheard two men talking about his mother.

"Skully, either I'm high as giraffe's pussy or Shaneequa is starting to look good," said Smalls while counting his money.

"Main-man Shaneequa has always looked good, she just like to play a little," replied Skully while taking a blow of cocaine out of a rolled-up dollar bill.

"Let her live Smalls, she already got one "Trickbaby" you know they say that she don't know who the father is," said Skully.

"Man, I don't give-a-fuck about none of that, I don't want to marry the whore I just want some head," said Smalls.

Hearing this conversation caused Calvin to have mixed emotions; the name "Trickbaby" sounded cool so that brought a smile to his face. But the rumor about a father he never knew brought on a feeling that couldn't be explained Rage! Calvin stormed to his room and slammed his door. Because his thoughts were all over the place he couldn't sleep. All's he kept thinking about was what was going on downstairs.

After thinking it through, he said to himself, *"Fuck the Ass Whippin' I gotta know what's going on."*

Like a thief in the night, Calvin tip-toed passed his mother's bedroom and headed downstairs. After reaching the last step he realized nothing was going on in the living room, so he kept it pushing. Once he got to the kitchen his eyes opened like two fifty-cent pieces. Through all the smoke, sitting at the kitchen table were six people, who all had "glass-dicks" in their mouths.

"They must be crack-pipes," Calvin thought to himself, *"I live in a Mother Fucken Crack House."*

After coming back to his senses, he realized that he didn't see his mother. *"She must've went to the store,"* he thought. So, he rushed back upstairs so he wouldn't get caught.

When he passed Shaneequa's room he heard a noise, so he stopped, looked, and listened. This time he heard a man's voice coming from his mom's bedroom. Moving like a cat in the night, he tiptoed to her bedroom door, which was slightly opened, and he peeped his head in. What he seen stopped his heart right where he stood. When his heart started beating again, every ounce of innocence that he ever had was gone. Skully had eight inches of dick in the back of Shaneequa's throat. It was at that moment that Skully wrote his own obituary and all other crackheads would pay as well. In the days that followed Calvin walked around the house wearing his emotions on his sleeves and a chip on his shoulders. Shaneequa's noticed the attitude change but didn't think much of it until one day while at the supermarket the pretty cashier lady said, "You are too cute to be looking so mean, what's your name handsome?" Instead of answering the lady, Calvin mean mugged her.

"Be nice and answer the lady," said Shaneequa.

"What's your name Baby?" asked the cashier.

Calvin looked the lady straight in her eyes and said, "Trickbaby," the lady damn near had a heart attack.

Shaneequa said, "I'm sorry ma'am, my son is just having a bad day, his name is Calvin."

"No, it's not, it's Trickbaby! That's how come I don't like going anywhere with you," said Calvin.

Shaneequa was stuck for a minute, not knowing where this attitude was coming from she told the lady, "Excuse me," then grabbed her son by the hand and left the store, leaving her groceries behind.

In front of the store Shaneequa leaned down in her son's face and said, "If you ever disrespect me like that again I will bust your ass!" His little heart was so heavy that he just started crying.

While crying Calvin's thoughts were, *These will be the last tears that she will ever see. My name will always be Trickbaby.*

Shaneequa still not realizing that she lost her 11-year-old son when she exposed him to Nightmare on Dick Street.

Santa Clause who happened to be riding by in his LX 400 Lexus Coupe, noticed Shaneequa who is his childhood friend holding it on young Trick, so he pulled over.

"Neeq, what's going on with you and my Lil' Man?" asked Santa while rubbing young Tricks head as he cried.

"Santa, I don't know what has gotten into him, but here lately he's been giving me attitude," said Shaneequa while holding her hands in the air.

"It's going to be alright Lil' Man," said Santa, "you want to take a ride with me?" While nodding his head yes, Santa Clause tossed young Trick the keys to the Lex.

"Santa, I got a few things to take care of so if I'm not home when y'all get back, just drop him off over Kim's house."

"Not a problem," said Santa knowing that because they were all childhood friends it would be okay.

After being treated to a pair of Air Jordan's and a meal of his choice, young Trickbaby was back smiling again. With plans of being the man, he would grow to be the grimiest of the crew. He was heartless and had no pics. Young Trick grew to be 5' 9" bow-legged with a stocky build. His brown-skin complexion complimented his hazel brown eyes. His gun and day ones were all the family he needed. Trick felt the world owed him something...

Thomas "Knock-out" Scott was raised by his grandmother Mrs. Shirly. Mrs. Shirley wanted more for her grandson than what the slums had to offer; so, she involved him in sports hoping that would be their meal ticket out of the projects. Thomas quickly found out that the only sport he was good at was boxing but didn't take it seriously enough to cash-in on it. The same projects that his grandmother hated, Thomas loved and couldn't imagine living anywhere else. Thomas never knew his mother and his father is doing a life sentence for a murder that happened in the same projects that Thomas loved. With the hopes of receiving guidance from his father, Thomas would go to Smyrna prison with Mrs. Shirly once a month to visit his dad. But a father can't raise a son from jail, so these trips was just hardening Thomas's heart. Spending time with his friends was the only thing that brought him happiness.

In the jungle everyday was an adventure, either they was on a search for girls or money. Thomas being big for his age was far from a bully, but very protective over his crew. At 14-years-old, he had the power of Mike Tyson, the speed of Mayweather, in the style of Sugar Ray. Thomas was usually quiet, but when it came to fucking with his boys, he became the loudest. One hot summer day while at the legendary Elbert Park that's located in the middle of the projects; the four were playing a two-on-two basketball game for money. They were competitive in everything they did, they even raced cockroaches for money. It was young George and Con against Trick and Thomas for $20 a man. The score was 28 to 28 and the game was to 32. All while arguing, fussing, and calling fouls, they've been playing hard for the last 50 minutes. The sidelines were packed with people watching these four young hustlers go hard in the paint.

While arguing one of the plays, the bully jealous ass Cain, walked on the court talking about, "Get off the court! We about to play whole court."

"Nigga, we ain't going nowhere," said young Con while dribbling the ball; Cain is now walking towards Con with malice in his eyes was caught with a one hitter-quitter by Thomas that put Cain straight to sleep.

Hustlers that were on the sidelines betting on the game, got Cain up and off the court so the game could continue. Young Con and George won the game, but the arguing amongst the four never stopped. While Cain who was a couple years older than the youngins was plotting revenge, they were planning their next big money scheme. While Cain became the laughingstock of the projects, Thomas was labeled a "Knock-out Artist" a handle he earned and will wear well. Young KO grew to be 6'2 and a force to be reckoned with. He loved his team and his projects; and if you wasn't from where he was from, you was in the way.

CHAPTER 4

Santa Clause the People's Champ

The sun is beaming, and the park is packed. It's "Southbridge Day," and all generations that were raised in these projects are here. The lyrics, *"It's a Hard Knock Life Instead of Treated We Get Kicked,"* by the rapper Jay-Z is booming out of the DJ's speakers. The kids are running from moon bounce to moon bounce; the grills are lit and filled with hot dogs, burgers, and ribs. The ballers are on the courts putting on a show and the gamblers are making it do what it do. They're shooting dice, playing Spades, Pitty-Pat, and even seeing who can spit the furthest, all for the love of the dollar. The older women are preaching to the young girls about "men" and the ins-and-outs of life. Mrs. Shirly is bouncing from grill-to-grill cooking while Joy, Shaneequa and Kim are trying to show their youth by outdoing the kids in double dutch.

"Santa! Santa! Santa!" screamed the kids while jumping up and down with their hands out.

"Calm down, calm down, it's enough for everybody; I got y'all," said Santa Clause while smiling and handing each kid a $5 bill.

Santa enjoyed bearing gifts and giving to the kids who were raised in the same project he was bred from. Santa Clause is a Kingpin-a bricklayer; he supplied the supplier's supplier. He was in the whole city's pocket. Santa Clause started selling fish-scale powder cocaine in these projects since the age of 12 and became a millionaire by the age of 17. He wasn't just respected in Wilmington, Delaware, but in other states as well. Every hustler in Southbridge worked for Santa one time or another and if you didn't hustle for him, it's because you didn't want any money. Santa was letting them "Birds" fly for the New York low. In his projects, if he ate, he wanted you to eat as well. When times were hard, he paid people's electric bills, did sneaker drives, and got the kids free haircuts regularly in his hood. Santa Clause is the people's champ. His model is *"No Kids Left Behind."* He moved out of the projects years ago, but these slums will forever be his home. Santa has three loyal friends that he trusted with his life. Dre, Marvell, and Obie are identical triplets and Santa's day one's. People who knew their bond would call Santa the fourth twin, the brother from another mother. They slept in the same bed, ate out of the same bowl, and played "hide and go get it" with the same girls. The triplets were ghetto-rich by association. Their job was to count money and deliver bullets; however, they moved in silence. Rumor has it that if you crossed Santa Clause in any way, you ended up swimming with the sharks by way of a black tinted out hearse.

The triplets were in the park and they were feeling all the love that is in the air, which brought smiles to their faces. A group of screaming kids took off running while scaring some of the adults in the process. As everyone looked to see what had the kids so excited and in an uproar, just smiled when they saw the Youngest-in-Charge members young George, Con, Trickbaby, and KO coming up the block doing wheelies on their custom painted, colorful dirt bikes.

After a half-hour of putting on a show for the kids, they parked their bikes and entered the park. While dapping the niggas, the young girls are blushing, smiling, and fixing their hair, all in hopes of leaving on the back of one of the bikes. The block party is in full swing and everybody is showing the young niggas love. This is their house, their world, and their park, and it showed on each of their smiling faces.

"Con look at George," said Trick while smiling and shaking his head.

Young George loved the kids and knew how to get them some memories that they'll never forget. George is surrounded by 60 to 70 kids who were all waiting in anticipation of his next move. He went into his pocket and pulled out a rolled-up knot of 100 single dollar bills. He counted 1, 2, 3, then threw the hundred ones in the air, making it rain on the kids who were going crazy! After going into his pocket two more times, it looked as if "George Washington" is having more fun than the kids. Santa watched as the kids went bananas chasing the dollars; he thought back to when young George was just a kid and chasing. It made Santa happy to see his little homie give back to the hood; he taught him well.

"Con, let me get at you, Baby Boy," said Santa while walking towards the grill to get a beef-rib sandwich.

"Whass the deal Big Homie, I see you flossen," said Con while giving his father figure a warm fatherly hug.

"You know it cost to be the boss to floss this hard; thanks for the gift," said Santa while holding up his pinky ring and Rolex.

"Mario said to give him a call."

Thinking about Mario brought a smile to Con's face. Since that caper, the Youngest-in-Charge has been blowing money fast; they split that loot four ways and gave the extra 10 grand to the lawyer Sam Guy for a retainer fee. None of them had any pending charges, but they were heavy in the streets and understood that lawyers, commissary, and bail weren't going to pay itself.

"Con, have you been looking out for your mom?" asked Santa Clause while taking a bite of his sandwich.

"Yea, I been getting' at her, but she's been getting' on my nerves; keep letting motha fuckas that I don't trust "in" and "out" the house," said Con with a serious look on his face.

"Main-man, you know she's hood and just be showing love, but since it's bothering you, I'ma holla at her."

"However, I don't want her wanting for anything; you're in the streets eating, so she eats as well. Con listen to me, when the lights go out, as they often do. It's goin to be your mother's touch, smile, and love that brightens ya day," said Santa, "now go grab the crew and meet me at my car. I got something for y'all." As young Con walked away, he thought about the jewel that was just dropped on him.

Santa had real love for his Lil' Homies, though he doesn't care too much about the way they got at a dollar; he couldn't knock their hustle. Santa knew that all's they wanted were the latest guns, Air Jordan's and gold chains. But he wanted more for them. Young KO, Trickbaby, Con, and George has made it clear to Santa that selling drugs wasn't their lane. They told him that selling drugs is stressful and that the flip took too long; because you're always on someone else's time. They stressed that they weren't standing on nobody's corner, they'd rather take money. Santa respected their wishes but watched their backs from a distance.

Back at the lab, Trickbaby is on his Nextel talking business while Con, George, and KO are trying on their new Gucci sneakers that Santa Clause bought them while in Atlantic City.

"KO shoot a hundred," said Con while shaking a pair of see-through red dice.

"Shoot it Nigga! Fuck is wrong wit you!! I got plenty paper and more where this came from!" yelled KO while pulling a knot of tens, twenties, and fifties from out of his pockets.

"Yo, Good-head Lisha is out front," said George while looking out the window.

"Y'all want some 'Head' I'm getting ready to call her."

Con and KO are at the craps table shooting a hundred and betting two; they're not paying George, no mind.

"OOOH, I like this, Lay; how long y'all had this down low spot," said Lisha while looking around, being nosey.

"Con, can I get a couple of dollars?"

"Fall-back Lish, I'm tryna to break this nigga," said Con while trying to hit his point, Lil' Joe.

Young George grabbed a condom from off the table then led Lisha up the steps. At the top of the steps, Lisha read the signs on both bedroom doors. *"PUSSY POUND: ENTER AT YOUR OWN RISK"*

"OOOH, what's that suppose to mean George; y'all crazy for that," said Lisha while entering in one of the rooms.

Lisha is 19-years-old, she stood 5'5, with a pretty face and a big fat butt. Lisha's project unit is where all the thots hang out.

"George, can you please pay my electric bill?" Lisha asked while putting her hair in a ponytail.

"Damn Lish, you gone handle me like that," said George as he's pulling the shades down.

"George, you know I've always had love for..."

"Don't worry about it Lish, I got you Baby girl," said George after cutting her off.

George had always wanted to fuck Lisha; he just wish she hadn't spread herself so thin. Last year, the hustlers in the projects gave her the "Best Head Award," and knowing that just made George want her even more. George now is stretched out on his back while Lisha is between his legs, giving him the "bizz-ness" she's deepthroating the hell out of his manhood. She's going ham on the dick, spitting on it, sucking his balls-George is losing his fucking mind. George had received head from a number of different females in his young life, but this work he's receiving today felt better than "pussy." The tender dick nigga is making so much noise that he didn't hear Trickbaby walking in with money in one hand and a condom in the other.

After sending Lisha home a couple hundred richer, the four sat at the kitchen table discussing a construction job that they were offered. A vacant building that is attached to a Dicks Sporting Goods needed some demolition work. Because the job consisted of loud noise, they were asked if the job could be done at night during closing hours. They really weren't into doing dirty jobs, but the Youngest-in-Charge members and money are like armed co-defendants; they stick together.

CHAPTER 5

The Lab

As the all-black tinted out construction van with Pennsylvania plates pulled out of the projects onto 4th Street, the driver KO looks in the rearview and sees three faces with looks that are as serious as a heart attack. The routine is all-too-familiar; it's the bottom of the 9^{th,} and it's nothing to be explained-Game on. As KO turns off of 4th and onto Market Street, young Con, George, and Trickbaby, who are all wearing a one-piece, all-black Dickie outfit, pulls their skullies down just above their eyes and put on their goggles. As soon as KO gets ready to whip the van into the alley that's parallel to the job site, the Wilmington Police, with sirens blaring, turns the corner in high pursuit signaling the van to pull to the side. As young KO pulls the van to the side, Trick and George jump into Plan "B" and pulls out their ratchets. Still, in high pursuit, the cop cars speed past and continue to their destination. Young Trick is happy that KO didn't panic and take the police on a high-speed chase.

Twenty minutes after getting their thoughts together, young KO whipped the van back to Market Street. Seconds later, KO turns off the lights of the construction van and pulls in front of the vacant building. He then takes a left into a nearby alleyway and the young hustlers went to work. Jumping out of the back, young Trick, Con, and George grabbed the wheel barrel, sledgehammers, bolt cutters, and duffle bags while KO is on the roof of the van taking down the ladder. Moving like a skilled craftsman, the hustlers quickly put up the ladder against the vacant building. In just the blink-of-an-eye young Trick was up the ladder and through the window with flashlight in hand. Trick was on the bottom floor and opening up the side door for his team. While young George, Con, and Trick were in a vacant building locating the area where the demolition will take place, KO was moving the van from out of the alley with the ladder back on top. Inside the building, they had found their mark, and with two sledgehammers Con and George went to work while Trick held the flashlight so they could see.

In just a few minutes, they broke through the wall of Dick's Sporting Goods and headed straight towards the guns. With the speed of Allen Iverson, they had cut wires, bust glass, and turned over displays, all while filling up the wheel barrel and duffle bags with handguns and assault rifles.

Trick, feeling his phone vibrate, quickly answered, "Yo," said Trick.

"Let's go," said KO. Sixty seconds later, they were back in the van.

Still hyped, Trickbaby yelled, "Motha Fucka! We Dem Boyz, money is the sweetest hangover Bitches!"

While being cautious and driving the speed limit, KO is smiling while looking through the rear-view at Trick, who's also smiling from ear-to-ear.

"When a wave comes flow wit it, I wouldn't change my nigggas for the world," said Con, who's thinking out loud but meant everything he said.

They were more than a team, more-than family; it was loyalty over everything; they are the Youngest-in-Charge. On one of the back blocks in Riverside projects, they pulled up behind KO's money green, smoked out 2003, Crown Vic. After transferring the guns from the van and taking off the license plate, they doused the van with gas and set it on fire.

While back at the Lab they counted 65 guns, five bulletproof vests, and unlimited ammo. It was them against the world...

<u>The Next Morning</u>

Hopping out of his black Chevy Impala with two breakfast platters,

Trickbaby enters his house through the back door; Shaneequa has been in recovery for the last 3½ years. When she was getting high, Trick held so much resentment towards his mom that he didn't listen to anything she had to say. Her actions had turned her son into a monster right before her eyes. They argued so much that some nights, Trick didn't even come home. He would stay at Con's or young George's; it was no use trying to stay at KO's house because Mrs. Shirly wasn't having that. She would always make sure he ate, then took him home herself. Today, young Trick is still learning how to love and respect his mom, it's a building process, but one he feels good about.

After putting the platters on the kitchen table, he called for Shaneequa, "Mom." After getting no response, he walked into the living room and noticed that the front door was open. When he got to the door Trick, saw that Shaneequa was on the front step talking to Skully. Trick knew that his mother wasn't back getting high, but what he didn't know is why was Skully still snooping around. He had already forgiven his mom for all the heartache and pain she caused. But still held Skully fully responsible for the mental torture he caused and vowed that one day he would rock him to sleep.

"Mom, you want some breakfast?" Trick asked while holding the door open for her.

"Oh, hey Baby, when did you get here?"

"A few minutes ago," said Trick.

"Well, Skully, I have to go, my baby boy needs me; I'll talk to you some other time," said Shaneequa as she followed Trick in the house and into the kitchen.

"OOOH Baby, that smells good; what you got for your mom?"

Shaneequa asked as she grabbed one of the platters and opened it, "OOOH, you know what your mom like, pancakes, cheese eggs, and bacon."

"Thank you, Baby now come give your mom a kiss."

Shaneequa walked over to Trick and kissed him on the cheek. Before Trick could grab his food and go upstairs his Nextel phone rang.

"Yo, Whass up Pimp," said Trickbaby.

"All Man, you know, just tryin' to see what-it-do. You holla at them folks?" asked young George.

"Yeah, I got at 'em. We in the game like EA Sports, get at KO and Con and let them know to meet us at the Lab at 12 o'clock," said young Trick while eating his food with his fingers.

Being from the streets, they learned early in the game that some phones could have bugs and leeches on them and to be aware is to be alive. A lot of Big Time Dope Boys fell hard fucking with them phones. I guess that's why they say, "The bigger you are, the harder you fall."

Young Trick is running the Rock; this is his connect so it's his show. They trust that he won't fumble the bag.

<u>3 Hours Later</u>

Trick and young George are sitting in front of the Lab in George's Audi S4, waiting for young Con and KO to pull up.

"Yo, Dula said that he got them fake IDs and driver's license for us; his connect at the DMV got them professionally done. We are in the system now, Baby boy," said Trick while fucken with the radio station.

"Yo, that niggas the man, he gets shit done fo' real, Trick we gotta throw that nigga an extra bone for that one," said George.

"Yeah, I know, he came through like I knew he would," said Trick.

As Trick runs into the Lab to grab the two duffel bags, young KO and Con pull up in Cons M45 Infiniti and parks next to the Audi.

"What's the deal, Playboy?" Con asked.

"You know what-it-do, sucker-ducken, and chasing checks," replied George.

"I know that's right," said Con while smiling.

As George gets out of the car to open the trunk, Trick is coming out of the Lab with the two duffel bags and places them in the trunk. As Trick gets in the car, he tells Con and KO to follow them to the park where Dula is at waiting for them all.

Dula is Trickbaby's older cousin, who's from the 2-6 projects; this set of projects is the grimiest of them all. Growing up, Doula was a thoroughbred, a young kid who always had it rough. After muscling his way into the drug game, he put together a crew of young bucks that were 30 deep. To these young goons, no rules applied; they made their own way with their murder game. The 2-6 Projects terrorized the whole city; in addition, with no mass, they robbed, stole, and killed. And on the strength of Dula, they had love for Trick.

As Con and George pulled up to the park, Trick notices Dula's black 750 BMW as well as a two-car entourage that he has with him. After parking next to the BMW, Dula walks over as Trick gets out of the car.

"Whass up cousin, I heard you young niggas is putten on for the city; you know the streets ain't just listening, but they watching now," Dula said as he gives Trick a tight heartfelt family hug.

"I don't know what the streets are seeing because we move like a ghost over here pimp," said Trick as he watches the rest of his crew get out of the cars.

"What you got for me?" Dula asked while giving Con, KO, and George a friendly nod.

While Trick and Dula's at the trunk of the Audi talking business, prime-time nasty, Slice and Spotty are standing in front of a 2001 Honda Accord. The four is not just a part of Dula's entourage, but also his shooters, eyes, and ears throughout the city. While KO, Con, and young George are posted up in front of the Audi with the eagle eye, Con notices Spotty "Gritten" on young George.

"Yo, why that light-skin kid over there keep sizing George up," said young Con.

"Probably because George is fucking his "baby-mom" but he can't be ready to die over no pussy," said young KO while gritten back.

In the middle of young Trick and Dula's conversation, Trick calls his crew to the trunk of the Audi.

"Is 85 grand cool?" Trick asked.

After receiving a nod from his crew, Trick gave Dula a smile, then told him that the deal was done. Hearing this good news, Dula waves over two females who are sitting in a blue Nissan Maxima. Tammy, who's Spotty's baby-mom, comes to the car alone. After Dula whispered something in her ear, Tammy went back to the Nissan, then comes back with a duffel bag full of big faces. After putting the money in the back seat of the Audi, Trick and Dula places the duffle bags of guns and vests in the car that the females are in.

After giving Dula some dap, young Con, George, and Trick hopped in their cars. As young George pulled off, he stopped in front of Dula's BMW and said, "Dula, tell your man that the Youngest-in-Charge niggas don't beef over pussy-we take money over here," then pulled off.

While back at the Lab to handle the breakdown, Trick realized that the DMV paperwork was also in the bag with the money.

"Nigga we just sold 60 guns, 28 AR-15's, 20 AK-47's and 10 9mm, 10 .40 Cal, and five vests. Who the Fuck is doin' it like us! We the niggas to see-we the only stars in this mother-fucken movie," said Trick as he broke down the bread 20 bans apiece and put five to the side for the lawyer.

They kept two 9mm's, two .40 Cals, and an Ak-47 for themselves. Usually, the rules are everything must go, but to every rule, there's always an exception, and this exception need not to be explained--guns.

CHAPTER 6

Will You Get Clean for Me?

"I'm so full; thanks for the treat Baby, you really showed mommy some love today. I'm just ready to go home and lay down," said Joy as she rubbed her stomach.

Young Con thought it was time that he spent some quality time with his mom, so he took her out and pampered her. He took her to the salon and got Joy's hair, nails, and feet done; then, he took her to the mall. Con told Joy to get whatever she wants and not to worry about the price. She picked out a Prada handbag with matching shoes, a bottle of Chanel perfume, and three Victoria Secret panties and bra sets. Before going home, they stopped at Red Lobster, and just the two of them had a feast.

"Con, I don't ask too many questions, but I really need you to be careful out here in these streets. You are my only child and I love the ground you walk on and if anything were to happen to you, I don't know what I would do," said Joy as she looked her son straight in the eyes and meant every word she said.

"Mom ain't nuffin going to happen to me, I'ma be alright, but thanks for slowing down the traffic from coming in and out the house."

"I know you just be showing love, but mom, I don't trust a lot of them niggas, and if anything gets stolen out of my room, it's going to be a problem," said young Con as they both got out of the car to go in the house.

Cain, Smalls, and Scully are sitting on Joy's step, watching the hand-to-hand drug sales that are being made up and down the block. Smalls and Skully used to be well respected in the projects. Both of them once hustled for Santa Clause until they started getting high on their own supply. Because both of them graduated from sniffing heroin to shooting dope, they can't get right and can't be trusted. Birds of a feather fly together; Cain, who's not shooting dope but sniffing it, is now running around with Smalls and Skully. Cain thought it was cool to pop perc 30s, which has the same effect as heroin.

Once his habit got too costly, he turned to heroin, which was cheaper. Now, he just doesn't have a monkey on his back but a Gorilla that's making all his decisions for him. He's stealing everything that's not nailed down; he's selling fake drugs, running off with people packages, and every other day somebody is shooting at him or chasing him with a knife. He's a junkie of the worst kind. Because Cain always makes something happen for them, Skully and Smalls loves that he's on their team.

Young KO's uncle AC who drives trucks for a living, is in town. Every time he's in town, he teaches KO how to drive his tractor-trailer in hopes that he will one day get his CDL and drive for a living. AC only wants the best for his nephew and doesn't want him to end up with a life sentence like his father. AC knows that KO is in the street because he just bought his grandmother Shirly a blue 2001 station wagon Volvo. KO likes the rumble that the motor makes when he pushes the gas pedal in the 18-wheeler. Riding this high in the air makes KO feel like he owns the streets. The way he's hitting the gears makes him feel like a kid in a candy store. After pulling into the parking lot of Bowlerama, they both hopped out of the truck to go in and bowl and shoot a couple of games of pool. Because AC always leaves KO with some "food for thought," he loves spending time with his uncle.

After a couple of hours of bonding and spending time with each other, AC set young KO down for a lesson, the same lesson KO's father didn't listen to.

"Nephew, I'm not going to preach to you, but I need you to hear me on this one. You can't beat the streets-they run too long. The streets don't lose; you can't beat them, there like Mayweather 20-0. Jails, institutions, and death are the only things the streets have to offer, and I want you to always remember that," said AC, "now let's get out of here."

Young KO knew these words to be true but also knew that it was going to take more than a lecture to get the streets out of his system.

Business at the bank is slow and Kim is looking more like a professional lawyer than a bank teller in her mini skirt suit. Kim has her long black silky hair pulled into a ponytail while showing off her baby hair. Kim's makeup is flawless; she's naturally pretty without it, but makeup just enhances her beauty. Kim's skin complexion is the color of a "Hershey Kiss" and as smooth as silk. She's 5'9, but her heels make her look like an inch taller. Kim's walk and the way she moves her hips make a preacher not want to preach and a teacher not want to teach. She is drop-dead gorgeous.

The bank executive Marvin opened his office door and, on the low, waived for Kim to come into his office. After counting the money, she had in her hand and placing it in the safe; she strutted to his office like she owned the bank. As she walked through the door, Marvin quickly locked it then pulled down the shades.

"Damn, Baby you smell so good you would think that Dolce & Gabbana made that perfume just for you," said Marvin as he pulls Kim towards him and started kissing her soft lips.

Without breaking the kiss, Kim brought her hand up to his chest and slowly pushed him back towards the desk. Kim hasn't had sex in a few months and her pussy is dripping wet.

"How bad do you want me?" Kim asked while unzipping his zipper.

"Baby words can't explain how bad..." before he could get the words out, Kim had his hardness out and stroking him.

As she continued to stroke him, Kim whispered in his ear, "Do I smell good enough to eat?"

"YE, YE, YES," he finally got it out.

Feeling like he was getting ready to explode in her hands, she released him. With no panties on, Kim pulled her shirt up above her waist and bent over the desk. Looking at how Kim's shaved and good-smelling pussy is spread Eagle, Marvin dove in tongue first. He licked her sweetness nice and slow, just how she liked it. Kim's pussy is so wet that Marvin could no longer contain himself. He slurped and sucked on her pussy so good that you would have thought he was eating watermelon because her juices had made it all the way to his eyes. After cumming in his mouth two times, Marvin put a condom on and slid in Kim's ocean real slow.

"OOOH, SSSS, AAAAH," Kim moaned as she took him into her love-box. In less than one minute, she became used to his length then started throwing it back while matching his every stroke.

In just five short minutes, the lame screamed out, "I'M CUMMIN! I'M CUMMIN!"

"Damn, Baby why you keep making me wait this long," said Marvin while handing Kim a box of baby wipes.

"Because I want it to be special for both of us; did it feel good to you as much as it felt good to me?" Kim asked, stroking his ego.

"Yes Baby, but please don't make me wait this long again," said Marvin while handing Kim an envelope with five grand in it.

"I won't," said Kim as she took the envelope and kissed him on the cheek.

"Sweetheart, you can take the rest of the day off; thanks for stopping by my office; I'll give you a call later," said Marvin while smiling.

"Look y'all, Porsha is outside talking to young George. She's probably trying to suck his dick for some money; you know she's strung out on heroin now," said Alisha while looking out of the door of her project unit.

"OOOH Girl, let me see, that's fucked up! That young girl is out there turning tricks, you know they say she be out the truck-stop on I-95 sucking them old White truck drivers dicks for money," said Tasty as she passed the blunt of Kush to Poundcake.

Alisha, Mo'Neek, Tasty, and Poundcake are all friends who are sitting around the kitchen table smoking Kush and gossiping about who sucking who's dick in the hood-but what they ain't talking about is who's dick they are creeping around the hood sucking.

"Porsha, when are you going to get yourself together? You are too pretty and have too much potential to be out here running around," said young George, who has real love, care, and concern in his heart for Porsha.

A year ago, while hanging out with some of the older females in the hood, Porsha picked up a Xanax habit and eventually graduated to sniffing dope.

"George, can I have $20, please? I swear I'll pay you back as soon as I get back from the truck stop," said Porsha while holding out her hand.

"If you think a dope fiend is paying you back, you can forget it," is what went through George's mind.

"Porsha, I'm not worried about you paying me back; I'ma give you these twenty-one's because I got love for you and don't want to see you out here dope sick," said young George while handing her the money.

"Thanks, George I love you so much," said Porsha while smiling from ear to ear.

"Porsha, I'ma get back at you because I might need you to do something for me," said George as he put the car in drive.

"I'll do anything for you Baby," said Porsha.

"Would you get clean for me?" asked young George.

"Any ting," said Porsha.

"Okay, we will see," said George as he pulled off.

CHAPTER 7

The Counterfeit Money

After young Con finished counting out 10 grand and placing it in his two front pockets, he tapped his sidekick Trickbaby to let him know that they were out. Both of them jumped out of Con's Infiniti and entered T.G.I. Fridays that's located in Darby, PA. The two purposely walked to a corner booth that has a view of the parking lot and it's entrance. After ordering two Corona's and three steak and shrimp platters, the two kicked the Willie Bo-Bo while waiting patiently for their guests.

"Trick whass up with these clown niggas keep running up New York and coming back wit all this knock-off bullshit? They fuckin' the game up! Pimp got all these young niggas running around wearing fake Jordan's, fake Air-ones, and them Acosta shirts, you know the shirts with the alligator on it. These slowpoke brain Motha Fuckas gotta know the shit is fake if they're only paying 25 to $50 for the shit," said Con while taking a swig of his beer.

"Yo ain't that your man pulling up in that new Ford Pickup truck?" Trickbaby asked while waving over the pretty waitress.

"Yeah, that's him," said Con.

AK is an African that's from Algeria; he's been in the US for 20 years and knows when to turn his accent off and on. If he never told you what country he was from, you would have thought he was an American. Knowing how and when to turn his accent off makes him a lot of money. Young Con met AK at the Trump Plaza Casino in Atlantic City, New Jersey. While at the Blackjack table, AK ran a scam on the dealer that only young Con caught. After AK peeped that Con caught the fifty-two fake out, he gave Con a wink. That night became the beginning of money being made and games being played between the two. After the three finished their meal, Trick left a $25 tip, then went to holler at the White Barbee who waited their table. Young Con and AK went to AK's truck to handle their business.

Ten minutes later, Trick Nextel rang. "Whass up Playa," said Trick while receiving the White Barbee's phone number.

"Time to bounce, Baby boy," said Con while walking to his car with a duffle bag.

"On my way Pimp," said Trick as he blew Barbee a kiss and watched as she caught it.

After getting in the car, Con tossed Trickbaby the duffle bag that consisted of 50 thousand of fake counterfeit 10-dollar bills. Young Con chose tens over twenties because tens were easier to push.

<u>2 Days Later</u>

Back in the projects, it's politics as usual. The summer day got the park packed as always. The young girls are out in abundance trying to catch a hustler in their mini's, boy shorts, and halter tops. Their stomachs, legs, and asses are out for the world to see; even the older ladies have their backs out. The basketball courts are in full effect, the ballers are running whole court and crossing each other up while thinking they are Allen Iverson or Jordan. The up-and-coming rappers are in the park arguing about who's the best rapper, Biggie, Jay-Z, or Nas. The drug dealers of all ages are rubbing shoulders and stepping on each other's toes, all while trying to see who can sell the most dimes, twenties, or eight balls.

"Gimmie the Loot, Gimmie the Loot. Gimmie the Loot, Gimmie the Loot. You Don't Have to Explain Shit, I Been Robbing Niggas Since the

Slave Ship. With the Same Clip. And the Same 45." Notorious B.I.G's *"Gimmie the Loot"* is blasting out of young KO's Crown Vic as he pulls up to the park and next to the craps game. Hopping out of his whip in a black on white Puma T-shirt, a black pair of Puma shorts, a white pair of Puma socks and a white on white pair of Puma sneakers, he yells, "Bet it Nigga!" while walking towards the craps game and pulling out two knots of twenties and tens from his pockets. With the tens being counterfeit though, it was young Con's caper alone. He still looked out for the cookout and gave his squad seven thousand apiece. The counterfeit money looked so real that you need a microscope to know the difference.

"George is that you!" screamed Kim as she got out of the shower and wrapped herself with a towel.

"Naw, it's Con!" he yelled as he close the front door and put his keys in his front pocket. "What's up Cutie, where have you been at, and why haven't you been coming to see me?" Kim asked while putting lotion on her body with Jergens Shea Butter Lotion.

"I'm sorry, I ain't even going to lie; I've been rippin' and runnin' and going nowhere fast," said Con while getting a glass of Kool-Aid out of the icebox.

"Have you seen George? Because I haven't seen him in almost two days and my baby would have usually called me by now," asked Kim as she's looking in the closet for something to wear.

"I haven't seen him, but I've talked to him; he's good; I'll tell him to give you a call," quickly replied young Con as he's running up the stairs to young George's bedroom.

"Thank you Baby," said Kim.

Con knows just where George is at; he's in North Carolina taking care of some business, but Con would surely let him know to call his mother. After putting George's share of the counterfeit into his safe, Con sat on young George's bed and pulled out his cell phone.

But before he could dial a number, Kim yelled," Con, can you please do me a favor!"

"Whass up Kim?" Con responded as he opened George's bedroom door.

"Come in my room, the door is unlocked."

After walking and Kim's room, he couldn't believe what is standing before him. Standing there in a pink matching panty and bra set was the most beautiful body he had ever seen in his 17 years of living, and the Dior fragrance had him in a spell.

"Sweetheart, are you okay?" Kim asked, bringing young Con out of his spell.

"Yeah, I'm Cool whass up," said Con.

"OK, which one of these sundresses should I put on, the yellow and white one or this black and white one?" Kim asked him as she pointed to both dresses.

"I think you would look nice in the yellow and white one," replied Con.

"I was hoping you said that one; my Baby got taste," said Kim as she grabbed the dress and stepped into it, "one more thing Sweetie, you have to zip me up; the zipper is on the back." After zipping the back of her sundress up, Kim gave Con a kiss on the cheek and told him thanks. Young Con has always admired Kim's beauty, but out of respect for George, he's never looked at her sexually and pray she never pulls that act again.

CHAPTER 8

Let's Get This Money

After coming back from the Lancaster Outlets and dropping a grip into the True Religion, Polo, and Nike stores young Trickbaby, KO, Con, and George decided to hood-hop all the legendary hoods in Wilmington. Trick and KO are in Trick's black tinted-out Chevy Impala trailing young Con whose in George's Audi S4. Though the sun is starting to go down, the warm weather has the town lit, and the people had the streets flooded. Turning off Union Street and on to 4th Street starts the beginning of the tour. The Hilltop area reminds one of the "badlands" of Philly. The Ricans and Blacks together cause havoc on these streets; everything's for sale, coke, dope, and weed, or Goya beans, rice, and patties; whatever your flavor the Hilltop has it to offer.

Riding down 4th Street, young George blows the horn at ES, Alfee, Lil' Iven, Jermain, KB, Shoka, and Shaq, who are all standing on 4th and Clayton chasing a check. Making a turn off 4th and on to Madison is the Westside and 5th the forklift is where shots are fired and hustlers dwell. Riding past West Center City, young KO waved at a few of the OG's who he knew from back when he used to box at the center. Block, CoCo, KB, Mo'Good, Fat Gus, and Manu are all standing in front of the center, flirting with all the beautiful women that are walking up and down their block. Making a right off of Madison and 9th Street, George whipped the Audi straight down to the Eastside. This side of town is why the murder rate in Wilmington, Delaware, is at an all-time high. These niggas will leave you stinking; they don't shoot below the shoulders, it's all headshots. Class, Beaker, Ranie, Mr. C., Harp, Ras, LB, and Fussy are all standing around and betting money on these two heavy weight niggas who are going blow for blow with boxing gloves on. This is the hood at his finest.

After riding through the Eastside, they made a left onto Church Street, then over to a small bridge to Governor Printz, which led them to the trenches- Riverside projects.

"Damn, what they having a block party out here," said young George, who's whipping the Audi through traffic that has come to a complete stop.

"Naw Babyboy, I don't think it's a block party, but with all this pussy running around, it's gotta be some money out here somewhere," said Con, who's trying to see what's going on in front of them.

George who is looking out of the rearview mirror see's Trick yelling out of his car window to a girl whose dropping it like it's hot to the lyrics--

"Drop Down and Get your Eagle on Girl."

"Drop Down and Get your Eagle on Girl," by the rapper Nelly.

"Pimp, I told you it was some money out this Motha Fucka, look at that big ass crap game," said Con, who's looking at George with dollar signs in his eyes.

"Main-man, them Riverside niggas is deep, it's money in that crap game. It's some 2-6 nigga's over there too, Baby Boy we about to fuck this crap game up," said young George as he looked for a parking spot. Before George could finish parking, Trick pulled up on the side of the Audi.

"Yo, what it do," said young KO.

"Park that shit pimp, we about to fuck these niggas pockets up," said young George.

"Yo, you strapped, right?"

"Yeah, why whass-up?" George asked.

"Because me and Trick about to shoot up Chester and grab some seafood platters from the Bottom of the Sea," said KO.

"That sounds like a good look; bring me and Con back a platter too," said young George as him and Con got out of the car. Alright, we out," said KO.

"George them dice still in the trunk?"

"Yeah," said George as he pushed the button to open the trunk.

"GIRRRRL, ain't that the boy from Southbridge that's fucking Tammy?" Star asked whose is standing in a group of about eight girls.

"Yeah, that's him," Toy quickly answered, "wit his fine ass."

George, who is wearing a black Nike T-shirt, a pair of black Nike sweatpants and a pair of black and white Jordans walks to the trunk of the car where Con is at. Young Con, who is wearing a blue and white Nike T-shirt, a pair of blue Nike shorts and a pair of blue and white Bo Jackson's said, "Come on let's go get this money," as they both walked across the street to the crap game.

Con whose Grandmom Piggy's gambling house is right up the street feels right at home. He knows all these hustlers, killers, and drug dealers, but doesn't trust none of them. The crap game is in the alley up against the projects wall. The game is lit, about 40 people deep and Monk is on the dice performing.

"Hey Baby." Is the greeting that Con and George received as they walked up.

"We been waiting to get some of that Southbridge money," said Naff while holding a knot in his hand.

"Well, come get it Nigga," said Con as he and young George pulled out a knot of 50s, 20s and 10s-with the tens being made for times like this. Monk has already been on the dice for 15 straight minutes and have hit five numbers in a row. His point is now 4 and niggas are betting like crazy.

"Little Joe!" Monk calls out as he throws the dice up against the wall. When Monk sees young Con he really starts to put on a show.

"Little Joe!" he calls out again.

Looking at Con, Monk said, "I'ma break all these young motha fuckas who think this shit is a game," as Monk hit his number 'Little Joe' and the crowd went wild.

"Let me fade him," said Con as he broadied his way to the front of the game.

"Shoot 50," said Monk as they both put their 50s on the ground. Monk rolled the dice and hit a six, with six being his point Monk bet Con and George both 200 apiece. In two rolls, Monk hit his six. His next point is nine and in just one roll Monk went out. Once young Con got on the dice three girls walked up towards the crap game-with Tammy being one of them. After giving young George a wink, he left the crap game to go "holla" at her. Young Con isn't playing no games, he's now shooting a hundred and betting 500. After hitting two of his numbers, Con checks on George who's still talking to Tammy. Con's point is now 10 and he's talking that big money shit to these niggas.

"Y'all motha fuckas can't Be Me or See Me!"

"Big Ben!" he calls out.

He shouts again, "Big Ben!" After rolling the dice up against the wall one of the dice stops on four while the other dice continues to spend for what seems like an eternity. When the dice stopped spinning and showed a six the crowd went bananas.

"I told y'all niggas that I run this Shit! I'm the Youngest-in-Charge, this is my Motha Fucken house," said Con while picking up his winnings from off the ground.

"BOC! BOC! BOC! BOC! BOC!"

Not knowing where the Assassin was firing from the females are screaming and crying while the niggas are ducking, hiding and running. Seconds after the bullets stop flying with gun in hand, Con is on his feet looking for George-who was stretched out next to a female with bullet holes to his chest and arm. Con immediately runs over to George who is gasping for air while trying to breathe.

CHAPTER 9

Breaking News

"PASS THE BALL! PASS THE BALL!" screamed Santa Clause whose watching a televised NBA play-off game with the triplets Marvell, Dre, and Obie. The Philadelphia 76ers are playing the Chicago Bulls, it's game seven and the Bulls are up two points with seven seconds left. Aaron McKee inbounds the ball to Allen Iverson whose being guarded by Michael Jordan. "Take 'em AI! Take 'em AI. NOOOOOO!"

"BREAKING NEWS: A 17-year-old male and a 19-year-old female were shot in Wilmington, Riverside projects at 8:20 p.m. The Wilmington Police responded to the 1200 block of North Bowers Street where they found the two victims with gunshot wounds-one being fatal. After being treated by the New Castle County paramedics, they were airlifted to Christiana Hospital. What you're seeing is a live video from the ABC Channel 6 News helicopter. On the ground the police are investigating the incident-at this point, we don't have too much information, but what we do know is a gun has been recovered and one of the victims street name is George Washington."

Standing in a state of shock and not believe in what they're seeing and just heard, Santa and the triplets grabbed their car keys and rushed out the door. With the triplets in the car, Santa is driving a hundred miles per hour. With blinders on Santa, only has two questions: Is young George the one still living and who's responsible.

<u>2 Hours Later</u>

Christiana Hospital's waiting room is filled to its capacity; George's friends, family and goons along with Tammy's people has the building in an uproar. There are a thousand questions in the air but not enough answers.

"Did he die?"

"Who shot him?"

"Why was he over Riverside?"

Alisha, Tasty, Mo'Neek and Poundcake are in the building. On the low, Alisha has been sucking young George's dick so much that she has now caught feelings. Mrs. Shirly and Joy are there in support of Kim who's crying uncontrollably. Young Trick, Con, and KO are on an emotional roll-a-coaster as well asking themselves, *"How could they have allowed this to happen to one of their own?"*

While everyone is waiting for the doctors and nurses to come out the operating room with answers, Detective Lacy and the Wilmington Police Department is watchin every hustler, gangster, and goon that are in the lobby. When Santa and the triplets walked into the lobby, it got so quiet you could hear a pin drop. Everyone's attention went straight to Santa who's eyes read *"Danger."* Dead or alive, after seeing this Detective Lacey knew he had to find out who George Washington was.

Dr. King and Nurse Mrs. Cornish walked into the waiting area and asked if they could speak to Tammy's mother or father. Mrs. Ward who is Tammy's mom and a crowd of 20 others rushed Dr. King. Kim, Santa and the others watching from a distance saw Mrs. Ward breakdown while crying hysterically. Tammy was dead on arrival from a bullet wound to the skull.

After seeing this, young KO, Con, and Trick could only hold their breath and wish for the best...The Creator isn't ready for George who escaped death. The first bullet went through his upper shoulder and exited his back while the second bullet is still lodged in his arm which is why he was in the operating room.

"Mom stop crying Baby."

"I'm good, I took them bullets wit a smile," said young George while hugging his mom from the hospital bed.

"George you got to turn it down, you doing too much," said Kim as she continued to wipe tears from her eyes.

"Glad to see you smiling pimp; you had me scared for a second," said Con while giving his best friend a hug.

"Thanks for cleaning me up main man, them pigs got there kind of fast," said George talking about the gun and money that he had on him.

After young Trickbaby and KO showed their love and respect in came Santa and the triplets. Kim who's still crying a river, watched as her son received a tremendous amount of love from four of her childhood friends.

"Young George, you still have a lot of people in the lobby who's trying to get at you to show their support, so I'm getting ready to blow this joint. But before I leave, on this piece of paper I need you to write down who is responsible," said Santa while handing George piece of paper.

After writing a name on the piece of paper that Santa handed him George told young Con to take Kim home because he no longer wanted her to see him like this.

When Santa and the triplets were leaving incomes Porsha with a card, flowers and balloons who would have thought?

<u>1 Hour Later</u>

Once Young Conartist thought Kim was done crying she started up again.

"Kim, it's going to be Ok; you got no worries; he'll be home in a day or two," said Con while using his keys to open the front door of the house.

Con knew that Kim was hurting for her baby, so she wouldn't be alone through the night, he decided that he would stay in George's room.

"Kim is it anything I can get you, maybe some hot tea or some soup?" Con asked while walking Kim up to her room.

"No Sweetheart, I'm fine. I just want to lay down and get some rest," said Kim as they walked into her bedroom.

Before Young Conartist could leave the room, Kim's tears started to flow again. Kim needing Con's comfort placed her hands around his neck hugging him and laid her head on his shoulder. Con held her tightly while continuously letting her know that everything will be alright. Seconds after she stopped crying, Con felt Kim's small, moist, pillow-lips on his neck and in a passionate way-A Kiss! Con understanding where this act could lead to, pulled back real slow then placed her in the bed fully clothed. After taking off her shoes and upon walking out of her room, young Con told Kim that if she needed anything to just call for him.

Pulling up to the crib, young Trick said to KO who's riding shotgun?

"Look at these two wack niggas pimp."

"What the fuck are they over there plotting on," said Trick who's watching Cain and Small's standing in the cutt.

After paying close attention, Trick sees who they're waiting on-it's

Skully, who's standing on the sidewalk talking to Shaneequa. In less than two seconds, KO watched Trick attitude go from being humble to complete rage and didn't know why Trick was triggered. However, Trick seeing Skully in his mom's face for the 3rd time brought back memories from when he was a kid. Trick got out of the car and slammed the door.

"Yo, what the fuck you in my mom face for; if I catch you in my mom face again I'ma Knock you the fuck out!" Skully who's now scared to death was looking at Shaneequa for some type of defense.

"Why are you talking to Skully like that? He hasn't violated me in any way and he damn sure haven't done anything to you," said Shaneequa who's looking like she's getting ready to smack Trick.

Hearing Shaneequa take Skully's side only made Trick more upset which made him go into his waistband and pull out a 9mm and put it to Skully's head.

Young KO not knowing where all of this was coming from jumped in Trick's face and asked, "What the fuck are you doing, main man you tripping. Give me that motha fucken gun!"

It wasn't until young KO intervened that trick came back to his senses. As Skully walked away, Shaneequa just went into the house pissed! Trick never told anyone about the Dick nightmare he witnessed as a kid; he just vowed to one day send Skully to meet his maker.

"Trick you need to tighten the fuck up, I know you are mad about George's situation, I am too but what are you tripping on the fiends for? The other day you shot Sweets with a BB gun, yesterday you smacked Jack and tonight you pulled out a gun on Skully who's done nothing to you. Trick for the disrespect you showed your mom you need to go into the house and apologize and get some rest. I love you man, I get at you tomorrow," said young KO as he jumped in his Crown Vic and pulled off.

What KO didn't know is that Trickbaby had some deep-rooted issues that could only be cured with professional help. He's just not filled with anger, but he's also hurting inside; and hurt people hurts people! Listening to young KO made Trickbaby feel bad. He knew that he disrespected his mom but didn't know how to apologize. The streets just didn't raise an animal but a monster.

CHAPTER 10

Who Shot George?

<u>Two Days Later</u>

"Hello Mr. Cornish, my name is Detective Lacy from the Wilmington Police Department, may I please have a word with you?"

Young George who is laying in his hospital bed and grooving off of the oxycodone painkillers the nurse continues to give him said, "Sure Detective, what's the problem?"

"You are a lucky fella Mr. George," said the Detective letting him know that he knows him by his street name, "I'm glad you pulled through, I'm sorry I can't say that for your friend Tammy."

Hearing these words and knowing Tammy's situation brought upon a sad expression on George's face. Detective Lacy catching this expression starts to lay it on thick.

"Mr. George, if not for yourself, please do it for your friend Tammy and her family. Do you know who shot you?" asked the Detective.

"I'm sorry Detective, but I didn't get a chance to see them," replied George with a straight face.

"You had to see them; you got shot in the chest, meaning the shooter was standing in front of you. Listen Son, we're dealing with a dangerous animal-a murder who may try to come back and finish the job," said the Detective while trying to use reverse psychology on young George, "listen Son, I'm not supposed to be telling you this, but we believe that the gun you were shot with was stolen from a gun store which links the person who shot you to that crime as well. Please help us help you so we can put this guy away forever."

"I'm sorry Sir but again, I don't know who shot me."

Furious that he didn't get the answers he was looking for, the detective went into his jacket pocket and handed George a card while telling him to call him if anything changed.

Young George who now has murder in his eyes is pissed! And can't believe that he was shot with a gun that he sold.

Boney's is a historical barbershop in the Southbridge projects and owned by three cousins, Lil' Rick, Donjuan and Locky who are all barbers. Today they are having a field day arguing about who is the greatest boxer of all time, Mike Tyson, Mayweather or Muhammad Ali. Like every hood barbershop you always have a professional 'Hood Analyst' who would argue you down about sports, music and politics. Then you got the ones that will really get *deep* on you and start talking about the slavery days, the Willie Lynch story and the new Jim Crow the book written by Michelle Alexander. The barbershop stayed packed, everybody that was somebody got their haircuts here. All professional cuts, you know, the kind that'll get an ugly nigga some pussy.

Donjuan who is cutting Charlie's hair is laughing his ass off about the boxing match when Tyson bit off Evander Hollifield's ear.

"Nah, but on the real," said Donjuan while giving Charlie a shape up, "is young George going to be alright?" asked Donjuan.

"Yeah he's good, in fact, he should be home today," said Charlie.

"I like that youngin, he's real smooth wit it. Is it true that he got shot over some pussy?"

"I don't know, but that's what the streets are saying," replied Charlie.

"That's fucked up if he did! When did it become cool to shoot a nigga over your baby mom? We ain't talking about your wife or girlfriend-But a baby mom, whose pussy is not even yours. These young niggas is wack for that," said Donjuan while brushing the hair off Charlie's neck, "yo, when you see him tell him that I said, "free hair cut" on me."

"A'ight," said Charlie while walking out the door.

Spotty is in the 2-6 projects with his New York Yankees Bucket pulled low to his eyes and serving a fiend. He's real antsy, his thoughts are cloudy and he is nervously moving about. For allowing his emotions to override his intellect, he knows that he has played himself.

Killing his baby mom wasn't a part of the plan; and for that act alone has Spotty spinning.

"Damn, why did she have to jump in front of the bullet," is all he continues to ask himself.

He knows that he has moved recklessly, because nigga's in his own hood is giving him funny stares and fake smiles. Even his man's Dula has disowned him; it's so much pressure in the air, he knows he has to get away.

CHAPTER 11

Home Invasion

<u>Three Days Later</u>

After coming back from the amusement park Great Adventures and dropping off a few grand to Tammy's mother for the funeral; young Con, KO, George, and Trick and parked in the front of Alisha's house just partying and bull-shitten. It's a warm night and the ghetto superstars is running up and down the block trying to get at a dollar while the females are standing in different little cliques, gossiping about the latest hood news and who's fucking who.

Young George is sitting on the hood of his M45 Infiniti talking to Alisha while young Con is sitting in the passenger seat watching 2-Pac's and Dre's "California Love" video on the cars TV monitor sound system. Young KO is in Alisha's house talking fly to Poundcake and Trick is up the block talking business to one of the many hustlers.

"What does your t-shirt say?" asked Alisha while standing in between George's legs.

"THE BIG DICK GANG," said George while leaning back so Alisha could read his shirt.

"OOOOH, why y'all got them T-shirts on? Y'all always gotta be different," said Alisha, "George I'm glad that you're Ok and out of the hospital, I couldn't stop crying knowing that my baby was laid up in that hospital bed."

"It wasn't that serious as it seemed Lish, the bullet that could've killed me went in and out. I could have left the hospital the next day, but they kept me for observations."

"Do you know who shot you?" Alisha asked while looking George straight in the eyes and really wanting to know.

"Lish, can we please talk about something else because I don't want to talk about that."

"Ok then let's go in the house so I can eat-it-up and swallow-it-down," said Alisha with a big smile on her face.

"Why you so nasty," said young George while feeling Alisha's ass.

"Nasty only for you," replied Alisha stroking George's ego.

"Damn Poundcake, you look good Baby girl," said KO while licking his lips.

"Thank you KO, can you tell that I've lost some weight."

"I can, but don't lose anymore because you look sexy as hell just like that."

Poundcake is a big girl, what one would call an amazon. She is sexy, beautiful and wear her weight well. Poundcake has swag, nails done, hair done, everything did.

"Poundcake what you home for spring break?" asked KO.

"Yes and I'm so happy because life can be so stressful at times; I'm just ready to wind-down," said Poundcake while putting on her lip gloss.

"I love me an educated female and can't wait until I find one," said KO while counting money and trying to impress Poundcake.

"Well, you ain't got to look no further because here I am," said Poundcake as she blushed and blew KO a kiss.

"Come on let's go upstairs," said KO as he nodded his head towards the steps.

"No Boy, get us a hotel room."

"Poundcake I'ma keep it real wit you, I ain't trying to make love, I'm just trying to fuck."

"I'm not trying to fall in love neither, but why do you have to say it like that?" Poundcake asked while reading *"THE BIG DICK GANG"* that's on the front of his T-shirt and wanting to know if what it says is really true.

Young KO grabbed her hand and led her upstairs to Alisha's bedroom. Once inside Alisha's bedroom KO buried his face into Poundcake's neck with soft kisses. While slowly moving to the other side of her neck, smelling her Vanilla fragrance made him suck even harder. Poundcake's pussy was so wet that her juices were running like the Hudson river. While softy kissing her neck, KO unbuttoned her shirt. After getting her shirt unbuttoned, he unstrapped her bra and to his surprise Poundcake had the most beautiful set of titties he had ever seen. They were brown, round and plump while caressing each one of her titties with his fingers. KO slowly and softly kissed from her neck down to her breast. Poundcake's whose now moaning to the beat of Ko's touch, backs up to the bed while pulling him with her. After laying Poundcake down on her back-KO French kissed each one of her nipples-sending Poundcake into a frenzy. She couldn't believe how he was taking his time and handling her body with so much love, care and concern. After slowly pulling down her Dior jeans and Victoria Secret panties, he passionately kissed her between her thighs until he made it to her Tunnel of Love. While gently licking and kissing her clit, KO was also caressing Poundcake's titties with his fingers.

Feeling like she's about to explode in his mouth, Poundcake grabbed the back of his head and moaned, Ohhh Baby, Yes! Yes! Stay right there-

Stay right there! AHHHHHH!"

Not ready to cum, Poundcake pushed KO's head up and told him to turn over. Once on his back, Poundcake pulled down young KO's Guess shorts and Polo boxers and couldn't believe how fat, long and pretty his manhood looked. Poundcake gently grabbed his man-ding-o in the palm of her soft hand and kissed the head while slowly jerking him back and forth. After a second of studying the beauty of his dick, she took him into her mouth and slowly went up and down while matching his every stroke with her hand. Young KO was now making all types of dumb faces while wondering if the pussy was as good as her hand. Like bobbing for apples, Poundcake is now deep throating the dick with no hands. Badly wanting KO inside of her, Poundcake got on the top of him, grabbed his pole and guided her soaking wet pussy on his dick nice and slow.

"SSSSS, AHHHHH, Damn Boy! This dick feel good," said Poundcake as she slowly grinding him.

"Take this dick!" KO said as Poundcake lowered her chest onto his and continued to slowly grind him until his dick was in her stomach.

"Damn Baby, it hurt so good," said Poundcake as she sped up the pace and used her chest as leverage to give it all to him.

"AHHHHHHHH, AHHHHHHHH!"

"Yeah take this dick!"

"AHHHHHHHH, I'm getting ready to CUMMMM, I'M CUMMIN! I'M CUMMIN!" Poundcake yelled.

"Me too! AH-SHIT, AH-SHIT! Damn Baby girl, you got good head, good pussy, you ain't a whore and you educated-I fuck around and wife you," said KO while smiling.

"Honey, you haven't seen or felt anything yet," replied Poundcake while rolling off him and waiting for round two.

"BAM, BAM, BAM!" was the sound of the bedroom door as someone banged on it.

"KO come on! Let's go, it's an emergency!"

"The police and ambulance are at your crib, let's go!"

After hearing these words come out of Trickbaby's mouth, young KO knew that this wasn't no joke. KO quickly jumped out of the bed and got dressed.

<u>10 Minutes Later</u>

Sirens are blaring and the Wilmington Police, Detectives, and E.M.T. workers are professionally moving throughout the house looking for answers. The State Division of Forensic are also a part of the First Responders. So, no one could enter the property, the front and back yard was sealed off with yellow tape. The crowd of people whose watching from a distance could only wonder what could have happened that would bring this many emergency units. Pulling up in young George's Infiniti, KO hopped out and beam-lined straight towards his house.

After running through the yellow emergency tape, KO was tackled by police officers who were standing guard. Young Con, George, and Trick who are running right behind KO. KO was now over the top of the police telling them to take their mother-fucken hands off of their family. The police are now shaken because the crowd is now screaming, yelling and threatening to throw bottles and bricks if they don't take their hands off of KO. The projects are in an uproar. After letting KO up from the ground, the police received the proper information that the house the police are in is

KO's residence. They then took him to the side to speak with him. While speaking with Detective Lacy, young KO watched as the coroner brought his grandmom out the house in a body bag.

It was a home invasion and Mrs. Shirly was raped, robbed, and murdered. Too much for his young heart to handle, KO just fell to his knees and asked God WHY.

CHAPTER 12

South Beach

South Beach of Miami is the liveliest beach in America and young Trick, Con, George, and KO are sitting on four rented scooters amongst a million females and niggas that flew in from all over the world. Needing them out the way, because too much is going on in the hood; Santa Clause treated them to an all-inclusive weekend in Miami. Staying at Lews, a five-star hotel that's located on Collins Street, the four sat on their scooters and watched the view as if it was a movie. On this street if you aren't driving a foreign car; someone from the sidewalk would scream for you to "park that shit" Because coming up and down this street, at three miles an hour so everybody will see you; are big body Benz's, BMW's, Maserati's, Lamborghini's, Rolls Royce's, Ferrari's, and Bugatti's. The Harley's and street bikes look like some shit that Batman would ride on. The bikes back tires are bigger than car tires. Females of all flavors-Columbians, Brazilians, Asians, Africans and Panamas are walking up and down Collins with nothing on but G-strings, bikinis', panties and sometimes nothing at all. None of the females were off limits for a hundred and fifty dollars you could fuck and suck all-night; and if you got swag and the gift-of-gab you could fuck for free. Real ones knows how it goes. Whatever happens in Miami-Stays in Miami.

"Yo, let's ride around Ocean Drive, they're having a bikini contest then after that we can go jump on the jet skis," said young Con as he started his scooter.

"Y'all go head and enjoy y'all-selves, I'm about to go to the room and fallback; I got some shit on my mind and need to clear my thoughts," said

KO.

"You want me to chill wit you Pimp," said Trick.

"Nah Babyboy, I'm good, go-head and get your fun on, I get at y'all in a Lil' bit," said KO as he pulled off on his scooter.

Young KO who's not feeling well mentally is still going through it. Knowing that he's responsible for his grandmothers murder, has left him with a heavy heart.

A witness reported seeing two men running out of the house but weren't able to ID them. Because KO's bedroom was the only room tore up-he knows the hit was for him. Young KO's safe had 60,000 in it, but because it was too heavy to carry, they left it. However, they were able to get 10 thousand in cash, a 9mm handgun, and two diamond cut gold chains; one with a Jesus piece and the other charm was a set of boxing gloves. The funeral was small and private-only close friends and family attended. KO's uncle AC has cut all ties, his reasoning was that if KO wasn't living a life of crime, his mother would still be alive.

Young KO's heart now beats revenge; he knows that what's done in the dark comes to light. The streets always talk and living this lifestyle, some-get-it and some-get-acquitted. Whoever is responsible it's death by torture. KO has vowed to be the judge, jury and executioner.

<u>Back in Wilmington Delaware</u>

Spotty smells death around the corner, he's moving in silence. The day has come for him to hit the New Jersey Turnpike and head straight to New York City. His whole hood has turned their backs on him and for their disloyalty he's getting ready to hit one of Dula's stash houses-then jump on the freeway. Since spotty was one of Dula's trusted little homies, he had keys to some of Dula's cars and stash houses. It's a quiet night in the 2-6 projects and Spotty pulls behind Dula's Land Rover in a black stolen Cherokee. After peeping the scene with two duffle bags in his hands he quickly hops out of the Jeep and gets into the Land Rover.

Fifteen minutes later, Spotty pulled up to the stash house in Greenville; this stash house is located on the outskirts of Wilmington.

After calling the house phone three times and not getting an answer, he knew no one was there. After letting himself in the house, he swiftly ran upstairs to the secret department and filled the duffle bags with 25 guns and fifty thousand in cash.

Pulling off with a Ronald McDonald smile on his face, he headed straight towards the Delaware Memorial Bridge the bridge that'll put him in South Jersey. Spotty sees the bridge from a distance but decided to get something to eat before crossing; so he stopped at the Chinese store to get some Shrimp Fried Rice. After cussing the cashier out for forgetting his Duck Sauce, he sprinted out the door. As Spotty opened the Land Rover's door to get in, a black tinted-out hearse with Atlanta tags quickly pulled up on the side of the Land Rover and two masked men with guns drawn and pointed at Spotty's head-told him that if he didn't get in the hearse his brains would be left right where he stood. After placing Spotty in the back of the hearse then closing the Land Rovers door; they showed a him a picture of young George at the Baltimore Aquarium standing next to a shark and on the back of the picture read--Revenge is the Sweetest Joy Next to Getting Pussy.

Cain, Small's and Skully are having a coke and dope party. Percocet's, Xanax and Kush are also at their disposal. It's a no clothes affair and the female prostitutes are running around the room butt naked.

"TAKE THIS DICK BITCH!" Cain yelled as he got the Puerto Rican Princess bent over and fucking her in the ass.

To not get kicked out the motel room, the four prostitutes that are in the room is practically competing with different sex acts to not be kicked out the room. Skully has so much heroin in his system that he's nodded out while the White girl is going wild on his dick with her mouth. The two Black girls are in a sixty-nine position-with Small's standing over the top of them directing as if he's filming a movie. Motel 6 must really keep the lights on for people because it's been three days and Cain, Small's and Skully ain't had a wink of sleep-and it don't seem like the party is going to end anytime soon.

Back in Miami, young Trickbaby wakes up from a crazy, wild night in the town. Club Champagne was being hosted by Miami's finest-Rick Ross. But Puff Daddy and Jadakiss were the ones who stole the show. Pulling up to the club in a rented Bentley, young Con, Trick, KO, and George jumped out like they own the city. Dressed in Gucci, Prada, Loui, and Versace, one would have never thought that these hustlers were only 17-years-old. They paid like they weighed and their fake IDs didn't just get them in the building-But also in VIP where they smoke Kush and popped bottles with exotic models until four in the morning.

"Damn that Brazilian chics head game was something special," thought Trick as young KO came out of the bathroom interrupting Trick from reminiscing to himself.

"Yo, get out the bed nigga, you know our flight leaves at four. Where did Con and George go?" KO asked.

"They went to drop the Bentley off to Carmelo," replied Trick.

"Yo, that nigga Carmelo is good peeps, he said the next time we come to Miami he's taking us to one of his parties."

"I'm wit that," said Trick.

"Yo, this plane is late as shit! We should have been in the air by now. KO pass me a pair of them ear-bugs," said Con.

"Hold on, I got you...my phone is ringing," said young KO.

"Hello."

"Hey KO."

"Who Dis?"

"It's Poundcake."

"Oh, what's up pretty lady?"

"I'm good, I'm sorry that your grandmother had to leave us so soon. But I've been praying for you and hope that you are feeling better."

"Thank you for your kind words, but you know what they say-What don't kill you, only makes you stronger," said KO while handing Con some ear-bugs.

"Well, I really miss you and was hoping that we could spend some time together before I go back to school," said Poundcake.

"That's not a problem Sweetheart, I'll be back in town before you know it-Just had to get away to clear my thoughts," said KO.

"KO, can I ask you a question?"

"Sure, anything," replied KO.

"Where do you see yourself at in the next five years?"

"To tell you the truth Poundcake, I haven't thought about that; I just hope it ain't six feet under," said KO.

"Not to sound preachy KO, but God has bigger and better plans for you and it ain't these streets. Baby, I know that it's a struggle, but you have to put yourself in a position to succeed in life. KO don't chase love, money, or success. Become the best version of yourself and those things will chase you."

"Baby just stay prayed up so you can be physically, mentally, and spiritually sound. KO, everyone has a purpose. You just have to plug into yours. See the Devil learns from our mistakes, the more we mak 'em and not learn from them, the stronger he gets. KO are you listening to me?"

"I hear you Sweetheart," said KO.

"Baby you will learn about yourself by tuning into different parts of your life and relationships. KO, I like you a lot and only want the best for you. I know that, I'm only a couple of years older than you and not perfect by far. But I do have a sense of direction. KO, I can help you get a job so you can build your credit if you like. Have you ever thought about going back to school?"

"Baby girl, thank you for your encouragement, but the only school I'm going to is the school of hard knocks," said KO.

"Boy call me when you get home," said Poundcake, while shaking her head.

"Ok Baby, I'll talk to you when I touch down," said KO, as he hung-up.

CHAPTER 13

The Truck Stop

<u>Three Days Later</u>

The truck stop on the I-95 freeway is bumper to bumper with eighteen-wheelers, the truckers are pulling in and out with different loads of stock. The drivers are filling their rigs with gas, getting something to eat from one of the many restaurants or just getting some much-needed rest from all the miles of driving. This rest area also breeds prostitutes, fiends and panhandlers-most truckers are more interested in getting a shot of head from one of the prostitutes or some coke and dope than resting. This is Porsha's spot and can't no one out hustle her on these grounds, rather it's conning someone or on her hands and knees--she's coming out a winner. She wants so badly to get out of this game, but the disease of addiction has her young mind trapped. From all the people who care about Porsha's well-being, she knows that she's pretty and has major potential, but still continues to let the streets swallow her whole.

The panhandler with the nappy beard and afro sees dollar signs in his eyes when he notices the truck that he's been waiting on. Two times a month this truck roars in. As the eighteen-wheeler pulls up to the diesel gas tank, the panhandler walks up to the truck.

"Sir can I please pump your gas? I haven't eaten all day. I'm not going to lie to you Sir, I look like this because I use drugs-But I promise you that whatever you give me I'll buy food with it," said the panhandler with a sad expression on his face.

Hearing the word "drugs" lit the truckers face up.

"I tell you what," said the trucker, "I'll buy you something to eat, plus your drug of choice if you can help me out."

"Thanks Sir, I'll do anything for you."

"Ok, pump the gas and I'll be right back." After pumping the gas, the two stood on the side of the truck that is now parked in the back of one of the restaurants.

"That's all you need me to do?" asked the panhandler as he waved "Skinny-pimp" over.

Skinny-pimp is Porsha's AKA.

"Yo, take care of my man for me Skinny-pimp, he's good folks," said the panhandler while nodding his head towards the trucker.

Porsha who's wearing a wig and makeup to make herself look older than 16 is still pretty as a butterfly.

"Hey Cutie, my name is Skinny-pimp and my friend tells me that you're looking for someone to make you feel good. Some tender, love and care," said Skinny-pimp as she shakes the trucker's hand.

"Beautiful as you are, I know you're not the one who's going to make me feel good," said the trucker as he puts his keys into his front pocket.

"Why ain't I Sweetie? I'm the best, why do you think they call me Skinny-pimp?"

"Well, actions speak louder than words," said the trucker, "but first, we have to get us some dope," said the trucker, as he handed the panhandler fifty dollars for his drug of choice and a hundred to Skinny-pimp for the dope.

"Come on Cutie," said Skinny-pimp as she grabbed the truckers hand, "everything is right over here," pointing to a van and the dope boy whose standing next to it.

After getting the dope from the raggedy-looking drug dealer they got into the van which had a table in the middle of the floor and a bed in the back. Wasting no time, the White trucker emptied three bundles of heroin on the table in one big pile-Then sniffed it as if the drug was going out of style. After taking two deep breaths, he grabbed Skinny-pimps hand and led her to the bed. The trucker then unbuckled his belt and let his pants fall to his ankles. Like the expert she is with no hesitation, Skinny-pimp grabbed his little dick and put it into her mouth. In less than one minute, Skinny-pimp was hearing moans of ecstasy so she sucked even harder. One minute-in-a half later, the moaning stopped and his dick went limp. The trucker had nodded out from the heroin-that was laced with Fentanyl. Springing into action, Skinny-pimp went into his pants pocket and grabbed his keys. While making sure not to touch anything in the stolen van, she hopped out and tossed the truck keys to two dirty looking bums as she got into the backseat of a stolen black Buick with the panhandler and the raggedy looking drug dealer.

<u>1 Hour Later</u>

The eighteen-wheeler that's being trailed by the black Buick pulls into two hundred acres of farmland that's privately owned by a young Black farmer named Akil; a thoroughbred who young George met at a 76ers basketball game. As the truck pulls into the garage, Akil comes out of his mini mansion with a Colgate smile on his face.

"Mr. George Washington himself, I see the panhandler skit has paid off like you said it would," said Akil as he shook young George's hand.

"Main-man I told you, this is what I do-me and my squad don't watch shit happen, we make shit happen," said George as he points to his most trusted army.

"You know what George, when I first met you, I thought you was a drug dealer."

"That's what they all think Pimp, but as you can see, it's a million ways to get money-selling drugs is just one of them," said George.

"Who's the pretty lady?" Akil asked with genuine lust in his eyes.

"Oh, this is my Lil' Sis and the one who gets the Oscar-because her acting skills are what made it happen," replied George while giving Porsha a hug. While young KO, Con, and Trick are taking off their fake afro's and beards, with a pair of bolt cutters, Akil is cutting the lock off the truck's back door. Filled from the back to the front of the truck are twenty-thousand cartons of Newport's and Marlboro's cigarettes-price value of over one million dollars.

A multi-agency search of a vehicle led to the closing of a popular Wilmington Street. At 7:30 p.m., the Wilmington Police along with the Federal, ATF, and DEA Law Enforcement Agencies were dispatched to Walnut Street. A forensic firearms examiner has all four doors of the Land Rover open while taking fingerprints. The caller reported that a suspicious looking vehicle has been sitting in the same spot for three days. Wilmington, Detective Lacy is being assisted by the alcohol, tobacco, and firearms in locating footage from the many businesses that sit along the busy street. If they can get video of the people who parked the vehicle in this location-it will give them a lead to this crime and many others.

The whole city is really excited and talking about the "Hustlers Ball" that Santa Clause throws every year at the Chase Center. It's an "All-White

Affair" and being dedicated to any and everybody who's getting a check. Santa is bringing in the rapper young Jeezy and DJ Cosmic Kev from the radio station Power 99 FM is going to be on the ones and twos. Philly, Jersey, and Delaware are going to be deep in the building. Females from New York, Atlanta, and Baltimore have already booked hotels for this weekend's extravagant event. Kim who's in the Gucci store wouldn't miss it for the world. The lame Marvin is treating Kim to a shopping spree. No longer needing or wanting his money-along with the guilt of creeping with a married man, she's been trying to cut him off-But the tender dick nigga just won't let go. The longer Kim holds back on the pussy, the harder the cheating husband slams his wallet in her face. It's only a matter of time before the lame really have to pay.

CHAPTER 14

Emilly is Questioned

<u>Days Later</u>

The cities barbershops and salons are doing numbers, the party they have been waiting on has arrived. The sow-ins that the females are getting look so good that the niggas don't know if their hair is real or fake. With appointments only, the front door of Boney's Barbershop continues to swing.

"Look who just walked in the door," said Donjuan as the other two barbers-Lil' Rick and Locky looked up.

"You know who it is, the Youngest-in-Charge," said young Trick as Con, KO, and George followed behind and greeted their three mentors.

"George we are glad you pulled through that nightmare Lil' homey; we were praying for your quick recovery," said Donjuan as he waved young George over to sit in his chair.

"Thanks for the love. But you know that I learned from the best-never let them see you frown, even smile when your down," said George while smiling and getting into the chair for his cut.

"I know y'all are going to support y'all mans party tomorrow night at the chase," said Lil' Rick while giving his client a shape up with the razor.

"SHIIIIT, be there I heard they're his guests," said Locky while putting a design in the back of his client's head.

"Yo, can y'all believe this shit," said Charlie, who's reading the Delaware State News Journal, "some White guy literally got caught with his pants down inside of a stolen van. When the police woke him up, he didn't know where he was or how he even got there."

"Damn Unc, looks like that nigga was on the losing team," said young Con as he gave Chalie a hug.

Chalie who's a Southbridge legend and someone the crew trust, respect and looks up too; works at the Port of Wilmington-The shipyard that brings and takes cargo across seas to other countries.

"Young Con don't lie to me. Is my only niece still in the streets getting high?"

"Unc, I was just getting ready to holla at you about Porsha; she's good, after her and George had a long emotional sit-down, she decided to get some help," replied Con as he picked-up the News Journal to read about the trucker.

After receiving 300,000 for the Cigarette Caper, they broke the loot down five ways. They each received 55,000 apiece while giving the last 25,000 to the lawyer. Pretty Porsha was tired of letting the long mean streets of Delaware beat her up. So, she allowed her baby George who has unconditional love for her to hold her cut of the money while she's at a rehab, deep in the mountains of PA.

"Yo, we about to be out, but I want to see all of y'all at the club tomorrow night; bottles of Cris on me," said young KO as the four left the barbershop.

Mount Joy Church is packed and the preacher has everyone's undivided attention.

"The Bible says that you must clean the spec out of your own eyes before you can clean the spec out of someone else's eyes," said the preacher, "you can't go trying to clean your neighbors backyard, if yours is dirty."

"Yes, Yes, Yes, Praise Him! Praise Him!" Mrs. Emilly shouted who has her hands stretched to the ceiling and praising her God. The whole church is cheering the preacher on "Praise Him" is what's coming from out of the pews. The band is playing and the church is cheering, "Yes! Yes!" BOOM! BOOM! is the sound at the front door as the Wilmington Swat Team came in with AR-15's and other assault rifles drawn. The people of the church are in a state of shock while some even fainted.

"This is God's house!" screamed the preacher, "this is God's house! Now why would y'all be disrespecting God's house!"

"Just calm down Sir, just calm down," said Detective Lacy while guns are still being held on the church's people, "listen up, listen up, where's Mrs. Emilly?" asked the detective while looking over the pews. Crawling from under the bench and scared to death, Mrs. Emilly raised her hand.

"We need to talk with you Mrs. Watson so please come with us." Confused, scared and with tears in her eyes Mrs. Emilly walked out with the police.

"I will be filing a lawsuit!" screamed the preacher, "church if you will please bow your heads for prayer because we surely need it."

After getting Mrs. Emilly down to the station, deciding to play good cop-Detective Lacy walked into the interview room where Mrs. Emilly was held.

"Mrs. Emilly Watson, we are here to help you out of a bad situation; just please help us because your freedom is in jeopardy if you say the wrong thing," said the detective.

With a scared and confused look on her face Mrs. Emilly asked, "Help you with what?" Detective Lacy then handed her a picture of a Land Rover.

Scared that something may have happened to her son, Mrs. Emilly blurted out, "That's my son's car, is my son Ok!?" yelled Mrs. Watson. Detective Lacy who's wearing a wire under his shirt wanted to hear Mrs. Watson make that statement again, "Mrs. Watson please look at the picture clearly."

"I don't have to keep looking at that picture, I know what my son's car looks like! That's my son's car-is my so Ok, I said!"

"Mrs. Watson, when is the last time you saw your son?"

"Yesterday," replied Mrs. Watson as rage started to take over her emotions.

"If you saw your son yesterday, then yes he's fine. And since you have been truthful up until this point, I'm going to be truthful with you. Your here because the title, registration and insurance of the Land Rover is in your name. But we know that it's not your vehicle. Mrs. Watson, we have recovered that vehicle and inside of it was some evidence that we know isn't yours."

Mrs. Emilly Watson is now looking puzzled; like she's just been played; but at the same time trying to think back to the last time she seen her son driving the Land Rover. However, with so much going on, her thoughts are failing her.

"Mrs. Watson, God must have been really hearing your prayers tonight because after you write down your son's full name, you are free to leave," said Detective Lacy as he gave her a pen to write with. 69-year-old Mrs. Watson wanted nothing more than to get home to her son.

CHAPTER 15

The Hustlers Ball

The Next Day

"It's Getting Hot in Here So Take Off All Your Clothes. . " The lyrics of the rapper "Nelly" is blaring out of the speakers as the females are backing that thing up to the niggas who's doing the same ole two-step.

"Philly, Jersey and Delaware-where y'all at," said Deejay Cosmic Kev as the packed dance floor screamed out their state. The all-white affair "Hustlers Ball" is an experience of its own-and the packed crowd is having the time of their lives. The party is in full swing and the line at the door is still around the corner.

"IS MY LADIES IN THIS MUTHA!"

"YEAAA!"

"IS MY DOGS IN THIS MUTHA!"

"WHOOOOL!"

Cosmic Kev has the crowd going crazy! It's so much designer in the building, one would have thought it was a fashion show. Versace, Dolce & Gabbana, Prada, Gucci, Coach, Louie Vuitton, Jimmy-Choo, Chanel, Polo-You name it, the females or niggas had that shit on; all-white everything. Some of the females gowns are down to their ankles while others are barely covering their asses.

Security is heavily guarded and the bottles are popping off like the 4th of July. VIP is on another level of insanity-only live men and exotic females are allowed in this area. This is where Allen Iverson, Ace from the movie "Paid in Full," and Michael Vick was at.

Santa Clause who got on all-white Versace linen was in VIP toasting it-up with the triplets and the 15 beautiful exotic woman he has with him. Bottles of Cris, Remy, Henny and champagne are being poured like it's running water. The Southbridge, Riverside and 2-6 Projects are heavy in the building. When the music stopped everyone looked towards the Deejays Booth as if something was wrong.

"We're getting ready to give some money away up-in-here. So, who's going to be the first lucky lady," said Cosmic Kev, "Amber White... is Amber White in the building? Come to the Deejay Booth and get your winnings!"

"ARE Y'ALL READY TO PARTY!" shouted the Deejay.

"YEAAA!"

"I SAID ARE Y'ALL READY TO PARTY! WELL LET'S GO!" said the Deejay.

"Bring 'em Out-Bring 'em Out, Bring 'em Out-Bring 'em Out. It's Hard to Tell--When the Barrows in Your Mouth-Swizzy!"

"Oh, that's my jam!" Poundcake screamed.

As she, Mo'Neek, Tasty and Alisha hit the dance floor. The song by the rapper TI had everyone on their feet and the ones who didn't know how to dance allowed their drinks to do the dancing for them. Kim, Joy and Shaneequa are in VIP sipping and nodding to the beat. Even the White-Barbee from TGI Fridays is in the building and on the dance floor shaking her little ass. The club is filled to its capacity and the line at the door is still around the corner. As the cocaine white stretch Hummer pulls up, everyone's attention goes towards the beauty of the car. Once the chauffeur opened the car door, young Trick, Conartist, Knock-out, and George Washington stepped out real smoothly dressed in all-black "Tom Ford" suits with gold cufflinks. The each of them had on one bracelet, a pinky-ring and a Rolex watch. The people in line are looking at them in amazement and wondering where did they think they were going dressed in black.

After receiving instructions, the 6'3, 290-pound doorman waved the well-dressed baby-faced hustlers past the line, through the door and straight to VIP. The attention they received when they hit the showroom floor was crazy! The love they were receiving made them feel like Rockstar's. Seeing Santa hugging and handing them bottles of Cris, let the people know that they were Somebody Special. Along with the Youngest-in-Charge seated at the 2nd largest table as well is Mario the jeweler, Akil the farmer and AK the African-This is the money table.

Deejay Cosmic Kev continued to play the latest club bangers as the barmaids played their part by steadily dropping off buckets of Cris. It was a mature crowd and they were partying like it was the NBA All-Star Weekend.

After throwing back a shot of the bubbly-young Con instantly caught eye contact with a female who looked to be from an Island he's never heard of. Her complexion is caramel and her eyes are hazel, she has the whitest smile and her hair is Brazilian. Her body is bad and she looks like her shit don't stink. Peeping what she was drinking, Con sent the barmaid to her table with a bottle of red wine. When the barmaid pointed back in Cons direction-letting the female know who sent the wine; young Con blew her a kiss. While young George is at the table trying to out drink AK, Akil and Mario, young Trick is whispering something sexual in the White Barbee's ear, because whatever he's saying has her smiling from ear to ear. Young KO and Poundcake are on the dance floor having a ball while trying to outdo each other with the latest dance moves.

Kim who is toasting it up with her childhood friend Santa looked good enough to eat; her all-white Gucci gown is fitting like a glove. Kim was 32 years old but didn't look a day over 25. Donjuan, Lil' Rick and Locky are drunk and laughing their asses off at each other. Young Con who couldn't take it any longer, decided to do what he do best.

"Excuse me," he said to the tropical looking female, "with all due respect, may I ask you your name? I don't usually do this but you are so adorable, extremely charming and the most beautiful female I've ever seen in my life. If I can just leave here tonight with your name, it would make this night special and one to always remember."

Not anticipating or expecting this babyface gentlemen to have so much Charisma, she looked him in his eyes and said, "Kelly, my name is Kelly."

Con is very selective in every way and about everything. He stay scheming, he will size a situation up from a distance-then attack. As young Con was about to thank Kelly for giving him her name; Kim grabbed him by the hand and led him to the dance floor. Young Jeezy is a no-show, but that was cool because the Youngest-in-Charge is the Shit of the night and Santa is the star in the sky.

A party wouldn't be a party if the bouncers ain't have to do their jobs. The triplets dressed in all-white identical Loui suits had the girls fighting over them like cats and dogs.

It is now pushing 3:30 in the morning and the party is starting to wind-down. Young Trick just left with the White barbee, KO and Poundcake is getting a room at the Hotel Dupont and young George is leaving to have a three-sum with Alisha and Mo'Neek. Young Con who's hoping to spot

Kelly, gets distracted by Kim asking if he could give her a ride home.

Blowing his chances of connecting with Kelly, Con said, "Sure Kim not a problem."

As the chauffeur was closing the door to the Hummer, Santa walked up and said, "Con make sure you get Kim home safe," while handing him a folded piece of paper-which Con put straight in his pocket.

After pulling up to Kim's house, Kim asked Con if he could come in for a minute because she had something to give him. Although Con wanted to say no but his urge to pee only left him with one option-Con told the chauffeur that he could leave, then he went in the house with Kim. After washing his hands, Con came out of the bathroom to the tunes of "Til the Cops Come Knocking" by Maxwell as Kim stood before him in a black two-piece lingerie teddy. Kim's pretty skin is flawless, as she grabbed Con by the hand and led him to her bedroom. Once she got him into the bedroom, Kim put her arms around his neck and passionately kissed him. Young Con who's no-longer able to fight off Kim's art of seduction let his tongue dance in her mouth while gently palming her ass. Kim's fragrance has now put him in a trans as he picks her up and carries her to the bed. Once they got on the bed she undressed him, then told him to lay on his back. While on his back, Kim kissed him slowly and passionately from his neck down to his belly button. The beauty of his muscle had Kim's pussy on fire! After gently taking his hardness in her hand and stroking it a few times. She took him into her warm mouth and sucked as if she was enjoying her favorite popsicle. Young Con has had his dick in more than a few girls mouths, but the was caressing and making love to his manhood was blowing his mind. As his moans got louder and louder and feeling the urge to cum; Con gently pulled Kim up and slowly turned her over on her back. While softly kissing her neck, Con smoothly helped Kim take off her lingerie. Once Kim's lingerie was off he took each breast one at a time into his mouth while gently rubbing her clit. After hearing Kim's moans of pleasure, Con slowly kissed down to her ocean which was now pouring. Using only his tongue he played with her clit until she was gently digging her nails into his back. Kim not believing how serious this young boy mouth game is. Her legs are now shaking as she moans out Cons name while telling him to stop. The louder her moans, the more passionate he licked, kissed and sucked. No longer able to take it, she grabbed his head and pulled him up. After pulling a condom from under the pillow-she opened it and gently put it on with her mouth. Now laying on her back, young Con positioned himself between her legs then slowly entered her wet opening.

"SSSSSS, AHHHH," her body as he slowly thrusted in and out of her love box.

Feeling Kim's walls collapse around his pole made Con go deeper.

"Ahhhh Connnnn," moaned Kim as he continued to slow grind her.

As he kissed her neck, a tear of ecstasy rolled down her cheek while gently biting down on his shoulder. Allowing Con to get it all, Kim is now matching every stroke. Feeling Kim's walls through the condom-let Con know that Kim got some good pussy. Now thrusting harder, Kim screamed out, "I'M CUMMING!" as her body quivered.

Now laying on her stomach, Con gently pushed her leg up then entered her from the back.

"Connnnn, Ahhhhh," moaned Kim as Con digs deep, "CONNNN why are you doing this to me! I'M CUMMING! I'M CUMMING!"

"Me too Baby. Aw, Aw," moaned Con as he rolled over on his back.

Kim rolled over as well but laying her head on Con's chest. Before Con could put together what happened, Kim was telling him that she loved him. Not believing what he just heard, young Con just shut his eyes.

CHAPTER 16

Rewrite His Wrong

<u>The Next Day</u>

The smell of cheese eggs, Turkey bacon, and French toast awakened young Con from an intoxicating sleep. With a confused look on his face, Con quickly put together how he ended up in his best friends mother's bed. Cursing himself for allowing his emotions to override his intellect, he quickly sat up. Trying to use a night of partying and drinking as an excuse, isn't justifiable enough to end up in young George's mother's bed. Conning and manipulating others is his gift but trying to justify his actions and run game on himself was a no-go. Young Con usually tries to live his life like a game of chess-with every move being a calculated step. Now, he has to figure out a way to rewrite his wrong without allowing Kim's good pussy to cloud his judgment.

After showering and putting on his clothes, Con pulls out a folded piece of paper from out of his pocket that read: `Kelly-call me at 609-655-7122 and call sooner than later`. Con just shook his head in disbelief.

After having breakfast with Kim, young Con left out the front door while young George is coming through the back door.

"They're trying to take my freedom, Trick, they're trying to crush my dreams; my vision is greater than prison. I'm holding court in the streets," said Dula who's in a nervous wreck and looking all around like a bobble-head.

Dula's lawyer has given him information that he has a warrant for his arrest-on the charges of murder, possession of numerous guns, burglary of guns and attempt of murder. Dula who's on the run from the Wilmington Police Department asked his cousin Trickbaby to meet him in a secluded area by the Brandywine River to discuss some important information before he leaves the state.

"Playboy understand this, I wasn't behind support or respect Spotty for shooting your mans over some pussy."

"His decisions have put me and my family in a fucked-up situation," said Dula who's talking fast and looking over his shoulders. Young Trick is allowing his cousin to vent.

"The nigga stole one of my cars and hit one of my stash houses, Trick."

"Playboy, the pigs have charged me with the shooting of your mans and Tammy's murder."

"Sound like to me the nigga double-crossed you; so you now have to triple-cross him," said Trick as he felt his cousins pain.

"Though I put a check on his head, I'm looking to kill him myself," said Dula not knowing that someone has already done it for free.

"Pimp, he's already swimming with the sharks," said Trick hoping that what he said will take some stress away because it was killing Trick seeing his cousin folding under pressure.

Hearing the words that Spotty is now swimming with the sharks is like music to Dula's ears. Knowing young Trick wouldn't accept his money, Dula went into his trunk and came back with something he knew his little cousin would love.

"Dula, where the Fuck did you get these from," said Trick with a look to kill in his eyes.

"When I was copping them choppers from you and your mans, I recognized this unique medallion "Boxing Gloves" swinging from around young KO's neck. And remembering where I last saw it, I didn't hesitate to buy it or this gold chain with the Jesus piece.

"Pimp, what do I owe you? I got five grand on me right now," said Trick while digging into his front pocket.

"You don't owe me shit Playboy; the information you have given me about Spotty "swimming wit the sharks" is enough. However, what you can do is check on my mom while I'm on the run."

"Say no-more Cuz, just call me when you get situated," said young Trick as he gave Dula a hug then jumped in his new Porsche 911.

The information Trick just received about the two individuals who sold Dula the gold chains fits the same description of the two who were seen running from Mrs. Shirly's house.

"Didn't them two slow-poke brain niggas know that the streets talk and it was only a matter of time before they would be brought to street justice," thought Trick as he pushed the Porsche through the city with lightning speed, *"their deaths wouldn't be business-but personal."*

After having a nice brunch at Warm Daddy's soul food restaurant that's located on Delaware Ave. in Philadelphia PA young KO and Poundcake are now at the Philadelphia Zoo. Holding hands while walking through the park, the two are having fun by telling each other what animal the each of them looked like.

"KO, I really enjoy being in your space, it's something about you that really turns me on; we have one-hellava chemistry," said Poundcake, "see that male gorilla over there, look how it's protecting the baby gorilla; that's how I feel when I'm with you-comfortable and protected," said Poundcake as she gave KO a kiss on the cheek.

"I'm glad that I make you feel that way pretty-lady, but I got that special touch on all my women."

"What you mean all your women?" Poundcake asked as she playfully punched him on the arm.

"Naw, I'm just playin' Sweetheart, but I am gon' keep it a hunderd wit you-I don't know too much about relationships; I was in love wit the streets growing up. However, you know that I was raised by my grandmom…so I do try to treat all women with love and respect-you know, treat women how I would want someone to treat my mom-who I've never met," said young KO while walking with his arm around Poundcake's neck.

"All that's so nice of you," said Poundcake as she laid her head on his shoulder.

The sound of KO's phone ringing broke their brace as KO answered, "What-it-do?"

"Yo, where you at?" asked young Trick.

"I'm up Philly, why whass-up?"

"Murder is whass-up, now get here," said Trick as he hung-up the phone.

"Come on, we out Poundcake, I promise to make this day up to you," said KO as they left the zoo.

<u>Later that Night</u>

Cain, Smalls and Skully's pockets are now looking like rabbit ears. The cocaine and dope party is over. The three of them are back in the projects and dressed like the San-man from the old Apollo. Looking like they're dead and stinking, the three are sitting on one of the project stoops plotting and planning on how to get their next fix. The young boys are in the hood shooting dice and selling the best coke and dope the city has to offer. Cain who sees one of the young boys hide his package, starts to fart while getting in position to strike. Pulling-up in her Nissan Maxima, Shaneequa waves Skully over to the car.

"Skully, when are you going to get yourself together and why are you out here looking like this?" Shaneequa asked with concern.

"I'ma get it together Shaneequa, I promise you that."

"Well, actions speak louder than words; Skully get yourself some rest because it looks like you been up for a couple of days," said Shaneequa with sadness in her eyes.

"Shaneequa can I get $20 please?" Skully asked while looking pitiful.

"I'ma give it to you this time Skully but you need to get yourself some help."

BOC! BOC! BOC! The 9-millimeter was singing in the young boy's hand as Cain grabbed the package and hit the corner. Hearing the bullets whistle past his head made Cain duck, weave and run like he was trying to get away from the police. Mad that he missed, the young boy screamed, "Yo that nigga is barred from these projects!"

"Whass-up Smalls," said young Trick, "you want to make $50?"

"Damn right Trick, what I gotta do?"

"Meet KO on the back-block, we need you to help us change a tire."

Needing some money to get his fix, in-record speed Smalls took off running to the back block.

"Smalls what took you so long?" asked young KO as he put on a pair of gloves then rolled a flat tire in Smalls direction, "put that in the back of the truck," said KO as he threw a thick chain in the back with the tire.

"Where's the car that needs to be fixed?" asked Smalls wanting to get the job done quickly so he could get high.

"It's on Christiana Ave.," replied KO.

Christiana Ave is a long street just outside the projects that doesn't have any lights or traffic.

"Damn it's dark out here; I hope you got a flashlight in the trunk," said Smalls.

The deeper they got on Christiana Ave the creepier it got.

"Oh Shit, I think I forgot to put the license plate back on the truck. Damn!" KO said as he pulled to the side of the road, "Smalls hop out and see if the plate is on this piece of shit."

As Smalls got out the truck, KO got out as well. Meeting Smalls at the back of the truck. KO caught Smalls with an over-hand right-the one hitter-quitter didn't just put Smalls on his pamper but put him to sleep as well.

Young KO quickly grabbed the chain from out of the back of the stolen truck and locked it around the bumper. The other end of the chain he viciously wrapped around Smalls ankles. After hopping into the driver's seat of the truck, KO pulled off. Young KO dragged Smalls body until his face was unrecognizable. As KO pulled to the side of the road, young Trick pulled on the side of the truck and hopped out with a gas can. Smalls who's "dead" and still chained to the truck-they doused him and the truck with gas and lit them on fire. Before jumping in the Porsche, KO pulled out his dick and pissed on Smalls face while telling him, "This is for the rape and murder of my loving grandmom-you Pussy!"

CHAPTER 17

Pit-bull's Trained to Kill

The pink red nose pit-bull has the white American pit-bull around the neck and shaking it to death.

"PSSSSS-SMASH, PSSSSS-SMASH," said Yola who's directing his red-nose to kill.

"Yola, who's from the surrounding area of Newark Delaware doesn't just train pits to kill, he also has the codeine syrup and Percocet 30's on deck. The crowd of 50 is cheering and betting on their favorite monster to win. Young Trick who's in the crowd has a $1000 bet on the red nose. However, he's just not in Newark for a dogfight, but also to holla at Yola. Because the American pit is hurt and scratching the owner of the dog gives Yola a nod to call it off. After collecting his money, young Trick called the county boy to the side.

"What-it-do?" Trick asked while still holding his winnings in his hand.

"Is that the boy Trick? Hay Babyboy, I see you out here getting some of this county money," said Yola as he gave Trick a pound and a half a hug.

"Naw, I ain't chasing no-money, but I am here to give you a little," said Trick who knows Yola from the famous elsewhere skating ring, "main-man this snake nigga in this picture raped and murdered my folks and I heard that he's hiding out in the county. If you see this crab in your travels give me a call." Trick handed Yola a picture of Cain and $500.

After looking at the picture, then looking at Trick, Yola said, "Babyboy, an enemy of yours, is an enemy of mines."

"Is there anything else I can do for you?"

"In fact, there is," said young Trick, "let me get a few of them Percocet-

of the door.

Knowing Santa's voice, Trick opened the door with a smile on his face. As Santa and the triplets walked in, Santa pulled out a .40 Cal from his waistband and handed it to young George.

"Lil' Nigga, you make sure that you show Baby-Wayne some love, he's the one that gave me the gun. He grabbed it as soon as you threw it. I hit 'em wit a couple hunerd, but you need to get at 'em as well," said Santa as he picked up the dice from off of the craps table.

"What are you trying to do with them?" asked young Con speaking of the dice that Santa has in his hands.

"Make it easy on yourself," said Santa as he pulled out a knot of benjee's from his pocket. As everyone walked towards the craps table, with a smile on his face Obie said, "Hold up! Nobody move and nobody gets hurt! Pay y'all niggas bill, that last jumper I shot went in which made the score 32 to 30," said Obie while holding his hand out and looking at young Con and KO.

"Man, that Shit didn't go in!" KO said as everyone looked at Santa-as if he was the ref.

"Pay like y'all weigh Lil' Niggas-that Shit went in," said Santa with a big Kool-Aid smile on his face.

CHAPTER 18

Can't Say No

Once Kim heard the front door shut, she quickly pushed play on the video camera. While Kim was at work, young Con called asking when and where was a good time for them to talk. The act of Con fucking young George's mother wasn't sitting right on his mental and he didn't want a piece of pussy to come in between the lifetime of love and respect the two had for one another. The Youngest-in-Charge members friendship ran deep; it was loyalty over everything. The four of them were raised without a father and in search of that fathers love-they found it in each other. The bond that was created was more than a father they would ever need. On Kim's lunch break, the two met at her house.

"Kim!" screamed young Con as he closed the front door.

"I'm in the bedroom, I just have to grab something real quick," said Kim as she hears Con coming up the steps.

After building up his confidence to tell Kim that they can't ever have sex again, the aroma of the Chanel fragrance that Kim had on hit Con so hard that he is now lost for words. Seeing how lovely Kim looked in her silk beaded mini had young Con hypnotized. Kim's chocolate beautiful skin is worthy of adoration

"Hey Cutie, what's on your mind Sweetheart?" Kim asked as she walked towards Con while putting in one of her diamond studded earrings.

"Kim, I don't think..."

Before Con could get out another word, Kim had her hand inside of his Polo sweats and caressing his God's gift to women. Hard and standing at attention, Con's dick did all the talking while Kim was telling him how bad she needed a quickie. Lost for words, Con just allowed Kim to have her way. After tasting him in her mouth, Kim positioned herself in front of the camera, pulled up her skirt and bent over. From the back, young Con passive-aggressively penetrated Kim's hole of overflowing juices.

"AWWWWW, AWW," was the moans and sounds Con was hearing as he long dicked her.

"AWWWWW BABY, YES! GIVE IT TO ME!" Kim yelled as she backed that pussy up to match Con's every stroke that he was delivering, "AWWWWW! YES CON, CUM IN THIS PUSSY!" Kim continued to yell as her orgasm of sexual excitement had her ready to explode.

"Damn Kim, this pussy is so good. Aw, Aw," moaned Con as he pounded Kim's sweetness just the way she loved it.

"AWWWWW, CON I'M CUMM-MMINNG! AW, AW, AW, I'M CUMMING!" Kim screamed. With the experience of a professional, Kim tightened her walls are Con's manhood in which sent him into a bliss.

"I'M CUMMING, I'M CUMMING!" Con yelled as he came inside of Kim's tight-fulfilling love-box.

"Happy Birthday to you, Happy Birthday to you," sang young George as Porsha walked into the drug rehabs visiting room. Not expecting a visit, Porsha's clown smile was bigger than any smile a clown can have. While giving her baby young George a hug, she is so over-joyed that tears are rolling down her cheek. Though Porsha was running the streets, George always knew that she was naturally beautiful, but what he was seeing today has him in a state of shock. Porsha is hands-down gorgeous, she has the complexion of a hot glass of Cocoa. She's 5'7" with softball size titties and fat ass. Her style is like fine-wine, Porsha got that Megan Good flow, but prettier.

"Whass-up Baby girl," said George as he's holding Porsha's hand while walking her to one of the visiting room tables.

"George, I'm so grateful for your friendship, your concerning words has motivated and inspired me to want more out of life than what our poverty-stricken neighborhood has to offer. George, I've learned so much about myself since I've been here. Young George the streets can never love you back. I'm now shooting for the moon and even if I don't make it, I'll still be amongst the stars. Baby fear is what put dreams to sleep and if people don't laugh at your dreams, then you're not dreaming big enough," said Porsha whose talking with authority.

Loving what he's seeing and hearing, George is attentive as if he's watching a teacher teach. As George watches Porsha, he also notices the many male staff workers who's paying attention to Porsha every move.

"Why are these lames sizing us up?" George asked talking about the staff.

"Don't mind them perverts George. They all want to fuck me when I leave this place; one time or another they all asked to either take me out on a candlelight steak dinner or go on an out-of-state vacation with them."

"And what was your response to the wolves?" asked young George with a serious look on his face.

"George the Porsha that was running around on them streets is dead. I love myself today, wasn't it you who told me how much potential I had? Well, today I see that potential and I'm worth more than a steak dinner or a vacation. Sweetheart, money and drugs no longer moves me sexually. I admit, the streets once got the best of me, but today I'm living off of experience and experience has always be my best teacher--I'll never lose again. Young George, I may be young but I'm all woman. I've been through so much in my life that most adults can't fill my shoes. George, I'm only 17, but I got big plans and Baby you will be a part of them," said Porsha while smiling and grabbing George's hand to lead him to the snack machine.

After another hour of allowing Porsha to take him to school mentally, young George let Porsha know how impressed he is with her recovery, gave her $500 cash, a kiss on the cheek, then told her to call him the day she's released.

The knock on the back door startled Mrs. Emilly Watson as she sat at her kitchen table eating her home cooked Sunday dinner. As Mrs. Emilly hit the button on her remote control, Detective Lacy showed up on her TV screen.

"May I help you Detective?" Mrs. Emilly asked as she opened the back door.

"Mrs. Watson, I shouldn't be here telling you this but unlike others in the department, I have a heart. There's some real important information that I have to speak with you about," said Detective Lacy as Mrs. Watson let him in the house.

"Mrs. Watson I'm going to cut straight through the chase; the Wilmington Police Department could easily charge you with the 25 different guns that was found in a vehicle that's in your name. However, because we do not believe the guns are yours, we released you from custody. The problem is that your son Dula hasn't turnt himself in yet, which leaves us to believe that he's on the run-leaving you with the charges. Mrs. Watson, my advice to you is to get on your phone and let your son know that he has one week to turn himself in. Mrs. Watson listen to me clearly, if he's not in our office in one week; the Swat team will be kicking your door in and taking you in with criminal charges," said the detective as he left out the back door.

CHAPTER 19

Taking All Bets

The Blackjack table at Delaware Park Casino is taking all bets and the Miami Guru "Carmelo" is at the table that starts at a grand. The businessman and his two shooters aren't in town for just fun and games but for business as well. Receiving the call, they've been waiting on, young Con, Trick, KO, and George dressed in all-black Carhart and ski mask down, jumped in a 12-foot stolen speed boat to make their way up the dark Delaware River. With the mindset that this is what they were born to do, the three laid down as KO handled the boat through the water, they all knew so well.

"Give me a piece of candy Trick," said young George as he watched him put something in his mouth.

"I ain't got no candy, Pimp," said Trick wondering why George would be asking him for candy; not knowing that George saw him "Real Swauvly" put something in his mouth.

After docking the boat in a pitch-black wooded area, Con grabbed the duffle bag as George shot two holes into the boat. Before making their way through the dark woods, they watched the boat sink. Twenty minutes later, they came to an opening of the Port-of-Wilmington, The Docs. This is where the biggest ships in America loads and unloads cargo from all over the world. After watching Homeland-Security make its rounds, with bolt cutters in hand, young Con and KO quickly runs to the South-wing gates and cut two big sections of the gate while physically rolling it back. Being fully aware of their surroundings, the two moved like ninjas as they dove to the ground and out of the way of oncoming headlights. After making their way back to where George and Trick was stationed, they sat in the dark until the signal was given. While waiting, young George went into the duffle-bag and pulled out four small boxes and handed them out.

After 30 minutes of watching Homeland-Security and the Feds move throughout the shipyard, the signal was given. From the west-wing the headlights blinked four times-meaning it was time to go to work. With a five-minute window period, with keycard in hand they swiftly moved through the darkness. As young George used his keycard to get into an Aston Martin, Con jumped into a Bugatti while KO grabbed the Maserati and young Trick whose fumbling with his key-card finally gets into a Lamborghini. With their headlights out, young George, Con, and KO pulled off towards the south-wing gates and stopped. Impatiently waiting and wondering why young Trick has yet to start the Lamborghini was inexplicable. After finally hearing the Lamborghini's engine roar, George, Con and KO takes off through the big hole that was cut into the gate. Still fumbling and high off Percocet-thirties, young Trick hits the wrong button which makes the car headlights come on. Seeing headlights coming out of the south-wing parking lot draws the attention of the Federilies who immediately gave chase. Thirty seconds behind the rest of his crew, Trick hits the hole in the gate burning rubber.

Now shifting the gears and making the Lambo scream, the Crown Vic the Feds are in is no match for the monster it's chasing. A half a city-block behind the Lambo, the Feds is now on their walkie-talkies and calling for backup. Knowing in a matter of minutes the chopper would be in the air, young Trick is now handling the monster as if he's been driving it for years. After hitting three short city blocks than an alleyway, young Trick had disappeared on the choppers and is now on the I-95 freeway floating.

<u>One Hour Later</u>

In a secluded area in the back of the Dover Air Force Base sits two 18-wheeler car carriers. As Trick pulls, up he notices the upside-down frowns that were on his boys faces has now turned into smiles. Carmelo who has a suitcase in his hand is off to the side speaking with young KO while young Con and George are in a group talking to Carmelo two bodyguards.

Two months prior while back in Miami, Carmelo got caught up in a tax-evasion scheme in which the Feds seized four of his high-end cars. GPS's being perfectly hidden in each of the vehicles allowed Carmelo access to know where the Feds were housing these cars. Knowing the cars were now in the State of Delaware and getting ready to be shipped to another country, Carmelo reached out to the Youngest-in-Charge who were all-game for the love of the "check."

"Trick let me get at you," said young George as they both walked to the side to talk, "you know that I pay attention to detail and Main-man you have been doing a lot of funny shit lately, your moving sloppy and that has never been you. Talk to me Babyboy, whass the problem?" asked young George while giving Trick a look of concern.

"I'm good Pimp," said Trick while trying hard to keep his composure.

"Nigga, you know that real eyes recognize real lies and we love you like cook food, it's loyalty over everything Main-man and if you can't talk to us about your issues-who can you talk to!" said George wanting to help his mans through whatever the problem may have been.

Young Trick wanted so badly to tell George that he has now picked up a Percocet habit but didn't have the courage to be truthful. Breaking their conversation, young KO called for the both of them.

"Is 400 grand cool?" asked KO

After they all gave KO a nod of approval, young KO gave Carmelo a wink, shook his hand and the deal was done.

After another 15 minutes of small talk, the Youngest-in-Charge was on to the next.

"Bitch, you should be thanking me for giving you a son, someone you'll be able to love even after the next nigga breaks your heart," said Dula.

Before hanging up the phone on one of his many baby mother's he left behind. Dula who's in the county of Conyers Georgia that's located 25 minutes outside of the City of Atlanta, is at one of the small bars stressed and throwing back shot after shot of Hennessy.

"I don't have an address Beautiful, I live on the road," said Primetime with nothing less than 10 grand in his front pockets and a 9mm on his waist. Primetime who is one of Dula's partners-in-crime is watching Dula's back while he's on the run.

"How a nigga like you live on the road and you look like money?" asked the beautiful female as the two are having a drink and talking slick to one-another.

Scotty's decisions have put Dula and his mother Mrs. Emilly in a fucked-up situation, knowing that if he doesn't turn himself in within a couple of days they're going to charge his mother with a crime, has him in a murderous state of mind. If only he could bring Spotty back to life-just to kill him again, he'll feel a lot better.

CHAPTER 20

Marvin Gotta Pay

As Marvin looks at the pictures of himself holding Kim in his arms and passionately kissing her on the lips has him scared to death. The only thought on Marvin's mind is his wife divorcing him and taking half of everything. Just the fact of her leaving with his two beautiful kids has Marvin willing to do anything it takes to make this situation go away.

Young Con, who is on another one of his crafty schemes is sitting in the passenger seat and pushing the gas on Marvin's emotions.

"You're movin' sloppy Marvin and for that you gotta pay," said young Conartist with an emotionless look on his face.

"Anything you want, just Please, Please! Don't let my wife get her hands on these pictures," said Marvin with tears in his eyes.

"Ok Player, you got 15 minutes to go in that bank and come out with fifty-thousand cash, if you can make that happen your wife will never get her hands on these pictures. In fact, I'll be leaving them all with you. Also, because I know you're in-love, you can continue sexing Kim. Just don't ever mention one word about this deal," said Con with a mischievous look on his face.

"If I get you this money, can you promise me that this will never come up again?" Marvin asked.

"Promise," quickly answered Con while thinking, *how could this lame be so green."*

As they both got out of the car, Marvin entered the bank while young Con went across the street and got into his new Cadillac SUV. It has now been 15 minutes and Marvin has yet to come out with the money. Now having negative thoughts that Marvin may have called the police makes Con feel uncomfortable.

After another 10 minutes and still no Marvin, Con puts the Caddy in drive and pulls off. While driving past the bank, Con hears a scream-in which he looks out the rear-view mirror and sees Marvin coming out of the bank side door holding a briefcase. Con stopped in the middle of the street, as Marvin jogged to the SUV and got in.

"Why did you pull off?" asked Marvin.

"Because I thought you was playing reindeer games," said Con while circling the block.

"It's all there and not a penny short," said Marvin while holding the briefcase in the air.

"I hope not Marvin, because don't no man want to lose their family over a piece of pussy," said Con as Marvin opened the briefcase to show him the money.

As young Con pulled to the side of the street, he went into the glove department to hand Marvin more pictures while telling him that he will never hear from him again. Marvin got out of the car happy, but with no intent to stop fucking Kim.

Young Con is now on his way to have a sit-down with young George about the love-affair he's been having with Kim and how badly he wants it to end.

"This lame as nigga!" screamed young Con as the Delaware State Police was pulling him over.

After a quick mental check of his gun being in the secret department and the briefcase under the front seat, Con pulls over.

"License, Registration and Insurance please," said the female patrol officer.

After seeing the face of the female officer, young Con thought his mind was playing tricks on him. It was the extremely charming and beautiful Kelly that he met at the Hustlers Ball.

Still ever so beautiful in her police uniform, young Con said, "Hey Beautiful," as he hands her the paperwork she asked for.

"Don't beautiful me and why haven't you called me?" Kelly asked with a sexy smirk and charming look on her face.

"Because I lost your number," replied Con with a bullshit excuse.

"What ever," said Kelly as she went to her patrol car to write him a ticket for speeding.

Five minutes later, Kelly comes back to the car and hands young Con back his paperwork along with a ticket that has a "phone number" on it and a message that reads: (handwritten text) You better stop playing and call me Boy." Then she walked back to her patrol car and pulled off.

As young KO whispered in Poundcake's ear, *"How good she felt"* he dug deeper and deeper in her warm, wet, ocean. While laying on her back with her legs spread eagle, KO is slowly and passionately making love to Poundcake's good smelling, good pussy, big boned beautiful body. As Poundcake slowly thrust the pussy back to him, she's moaning KO's name and telling him to go faster and deeper.

"AWWWWWW," she loudly moaned as KO lifted her legs over his arms and strokes it like a porn star.

"Baby it feels so good," she cried as she tightened her walls, dug her nails into his back and then creamed all over his dick.

Feeling the urge to cum, young KO pulled his long, fat manhood from out of her juices and came all over her titties. From the work he put in, KO whose now exhausted rolls over on his back, as Poundcake quickly runs to the shower.

While home on college break, Poundcake is doing an internship at the New Castle County Courthouse and can't be late. Born Leena Robinson, whose dad gave the nickname Poundcake because she was a chubby baby; was born and raised in the projects. However, because her parents were well off, they moved four streets over to the townhouses which are still considered the Southbridge Projects. Now in-love, KO is trying to think of a loving and caring way to tell Poundcake that he's in-love and wants their relationship to now be exclusive.

"She has morals, values, brains and she's trustworthy; why wouldn't I make her wifey," thought KO.

After getting out of the shower, Poundcake is now in her walk-in closet putting on her DKNY panty and bra set.

"KO, why are these young boys so jealous of one another and killing each other over pennies?" Poundcake asked with a sad expression on her face.

"Because niggas are broke, hungry and walking around wit a chip on their shoulders-it's so bad that the hate, hunger and frustration be seeping out of niggas pores like sweat," said KO with a nonchalant attitude.

"I'm just glad that you are mature," said Poundcake not knowing that she's in-love with a killer, "see grown men will try to unite, while little boys will try to compete," said Poundcake as she's now putting on her heels.

"And you know what, being broke is not an excuse, because I've learned that-being broke is temporary, but being poor is internal," said Poundcake as she grabbed her keys and his hand for them to leave.

CHAPTER 21

Trick Loses

<u>2 Days Later</u>

After losing $20,000 between the 21 Blackjack and craps tables, young Trick is now sitting at one of the small bars inside the Dover Downs Casino. After throwing back numerous shots of Remy Martin, Trick is now arguing with the bartender about how he believes the craps table cheated him. Trick has always walked around with a chip on his shoulder. But now since he's been eating Percocet-thirties, his attitude has been zero to a hundred. The more he hangs-out and Fucks the White-Barbee in every hole but her ears, the worse his habit gets. While walking back to the craps table, Trick's phone rings.

"If it ain't about money, then right now ain't a good time," said Trick as he put his ear to the receiver and meant every word he said.

"Well, you might want to hear this," said Yola, "I got the drop on Cain." Not needing to hear anymore, Trick direction has now turnt towards the front door.

"Listen to me," said young Trick, "do you have any Perc's?"

"Unlimited, I also got some raw heroin that's literally killing people," said Yola as he watches Cain from a distance.

"Ok, give me one hour, but in the meantime, do what ever you have to do to lure Cain into a secluded area," said Trick while talking reckless and not respecting the number one phone rule.

An hour and twenty minutes later, young KO and Trick pulls up to a ran down vacant building that's surrounded by other vacant warehouses. As the two got out of the black stolen Honda Civic, Yola exited the vacant building.

"Is the coward in the building?" KO asked as he wipes his sweaty hands off on his black denim Guess jeans.

"Yeah, he's in there, he thinks that he's getting ready to help me cut this dope-that has now killed four people," answered Yola as he points to the black Phillies bookbag that's hanging from his shoulder.

After whispering something in Yola's ear, young Trick and KO walked into the building as Yola went in the opposite direction.

"What's up Cain," said Trick as they both entered the room Cain was in.

"I see y'all here to get some of that fire that Yola got," said Cain as he shook Trick's hand.

As Cain went to shake KO's hand, KO stole him with the one-hitter-quitter that put Cain to sleep. But before hitting the floor, KO caught him with a mean left which now woke Cain up. He's now laying on the floor with his eyes open-but snoring. When Cain became conscious, he was tied to a chair and being smacked by young Trickbaby.

"Why did you rape and murder the only lady that ever loved me? Cain-you violated the number one rule, mothers and kids are off limits. If you would have just robbed me, I would have respected your hustle and charged it to the game. You would have probably ended up in a wheelchair, but I may have spared you your life. Now for your acts, you have signed, sealed and delivered your own Death Certificate," said KO as Trick opened the door for Yola who came in with the red-nosed pit-bull. As Cain cries, he's blaming Smalls for everything that happened to young KO's grandmother. Lost in the moment, KO gives Yola the wink whose standing four feet in front of Cain and holding the red-nosed by the leash while ordering the beast to smash!

"SSSSS-SMASH, SSSSS-SMASH," orders Yola as the pit-bull is foaming out the mouth, barking and trying desperately to get to its prey.

"SSSSS-SMASH," Cain whose still crying a river has now shitted and pissed on himself.

"SSSSS-SMASH," directed Yola as he let the red-nosed go. Wasting no time, the pit-bull took two steps and leaped up, grabbing Cain by the neck and shook uncontrollably. Trained to kill, while receiving orders from its owner to smash, the pit-bull has Cain screaming while going in and out of consciousness. When Yola pulled the red-nosed from off of Cain. The pit still had a chunk of Cain's neck in its mouth. Not wasting any more time, young KO pulled out his .40 Cal and shot Cain in the head-giving him a wiggie. As KO dug into his pocket to pay Yola for the drop, young Trick pulled out his 9mm and shot the pit-bull in the head. With a confused look on his face, Yola raised both hands up as if to say why. "BOC! BOC!" As another 9mm bullet laid Yola right next to mans best friend-his dog.

Looking at Trick, KO also asked, "Why?"

"Because I don't trust him. Do you?" Trick asked as he grabbed the Phillies bookbag from off of the floor, then left the building.

Sirens blaring and blowing his horn Detective Lacy is cursing the traffic for not respecting the emergency of a police cruiser. With no time to waste, he presses the gas as he silently prays that he makes it to his destination on time.

"If only the Basterd would have done the right thing," thought the detective as he ran a red light and headed straight to the poverty-stricken neighborhood. Unmarked cop vehicles had the street blocked off while the

SWAT Team who carried AK's, .40 Cals and 9mm's had the house surrounded and waiting for their signal.

As Detective Lacy pulled up, he noticed that the SWAT Team is fully geared and in position to strike. Quickly opening the door, the detective jumped out of the cruiser screaming, "NOOOO!" as the signal was given.

"BOOM! BOOM!" Was the sound of the door as the SWAT Team busted in and looking to murder anything that moved. In her favorite part of the house "the kitchen" is where Mrs. Emilly is at cooking a meal for the homeless who attends her church. The noise the SWAT team made coming through the door, along with the AK's pointing in her face-literally scared her to death. When Detective Lacy bust through the door, Mrs. Emilly had already fainted and was now stretched out on the floor going into cardiac arrest.

"There's been a crisis, someone call the ambulance Now!" screamed the detective while given Mrs. Emilly CPR, "Tom, you didn't have to do it, she would have surrendered peacefully," said Detective Lacy while pointing his finger into the sergeant face.

"It was an order that was signed by the judge Detective; it was out of my hands."

Forty-five minutes later, Mrs. Emilly was pronounced dead at the Christiana Hospital. The cause of death was a heart attack. Mrs. Emilly's heart could no-longer stand the pressure that the corrupt streets directed her way. Turning 70, Mrs. Emilly died on her birthday.

"That God-Damn Dula! If only he had turned himself in. I'm not going to rest until he's in cuffs or buried six-feet deep," said Detective Lacy with hate in his blood.

CHAPTER 22

Baby Wayne is Surrounded

<u>Days Later</u>

"The police got the young boy Baby Wayne surrounded up the street," said Chalie as he walked into the barbershop with a hand full of money.

"That young boy drives a different stolen car every day; I knew the pigs were going to run-down on him sooner or later," said Lil' Rick as he's cutting one of his client's hair.

"Chalie, where you get all that money from?" Locky asked as he waved Chalie to come sit in his chair.

"I hit the lottery," replied Chalie with a smile on his face.

"Stop lying Nigga, you ain't hit no God-Damn lottery," said Locky.

"You know I can't lie, I go to church," said Chalie while still smiling.

"A lie don't care who tell it," said Donjuan as they all broke out laughing.

Chalie had just got paid for his part in the car heist. He was the one who gave the signal, by blinking his headlights four times. The part he played got him 10 grand. Working at the Port-of-Wilmington got Chalie paid in more ways than one.

"Did y'all see the news last night?" Donjuan asked as he stopped cutting to be sure he had everyone's attention, "the police identified one of the two bodies that were found in that vacant building as Cain."

"Are you serious?" asked Locky.

"Serious as a heart attack," quickly responded Donjuan.

"That nigga was doing too much, I knew his clock was about to stop," said Lil' Rick while shaking his head.

"First it was Smalls, now Cain, who's next? Because you know they say that people die in threes," said Locky.

"You know Skully's on that team, that nigga better go check into somebody's rehab before he ends up crossing someone-if he hasn't already," said Donjuan.

"Chalie how is your niece Porsha doing?" Locky asked while dying Chalie's beard.

"She's doing marvelous, me and young George went to see her yesterday. She said, failure is a bruise, not a tattoo; I'm telling y'all, she's focused, intelligent and beautiful. These slow-poke-brain niggas ain't going to know how to handle her this round," said Chalie, happy that his only niece made it from out of the jaws of the hungry streets.

"Shit, these young niggas is already fumbling the ball; they think because they pop pills, they're a better junkie than the ones that's sniffing dope or smoking coke," said Locky.

"Rather you are selling drugs, using drugs, or robbing niggas to get drugs; it's all drug related and neither is better than the other-the justice system looks at them all the same-JAIL," said Lil' Rick who is happy to hear that Porsha is recovering well.

"Man, these streets are messy; the city is talking about how Dula literally left his mom for dead-all he had to do was turn his self in and make bail. But instead, he let the pigs run down on her; now that's fucked up," said Donjuan as Alisha runs into the barbershop screaming.

"Baby Wayne just rammed a police cruiser in a black stolen Honda Civic, now he's taking them on a high-speed chase."

<u>Later that Night</u>

"DROP IT LIKE IT'S HOT-DROP IT LIKE IT'S HOT" The song by Snoop Dog and Pharrell is blaring out of the speakers of the famous Elsewhere skating rink. The building is filled to its capacity and the hustlers, ballers and shot callers are competing for the females attention. One of Delaware's finest, the author of "Bloody Money" Le'Andre Prince is on the floor and backward skating to the beat. Pretty women from all-walks of life are on their skates and dancing-as if skating is their favorite hobby.

The Youngest-in-Charge has just entered the building and they didn't come to skate. With sneakers on their feet, knots of money in their pockets and guns on their waist; they're headed straight towards the bathroom where the biggest crap game of the week is being held. Dressed identical and all wearing white skates, Alisha, Mo'Neek, Poundcake and Tasty all screamed, "Southbridge!" as they are line-skating while doing the same dance moves. When they entered the bathroom, the smell of Kush is heavy in the air and big faces are all over the floor.

The small bathroom is deep with people from all-sides of the city. The boy "No-change" is on the dice and just the person that Trickbaby want to see. As the Youngest-in-Charge are receiving much love from many and funny stares from a few; No-change is a jack-of-all-trades and a master chef who has Gucci dialogue. He can sell water to a whale and salt to a snail. He's not just Dula's mans, but also a Riverside Project nigga to the core.

"No-change, let me get at you Main-man, let's go talk money," said young Trick as he gave No-change a nod towards the bathroom door.

The duffle bag that young Trick took from Yola consisted of 1,000 Percocet-thirties and three ounces of raw heroin. Because the dope is too pure to be put on the streets, the master chef was asked to make the dope do what it do.

Young Con point is six and the pot is worth $5,000. As he shook the dice, young KO dropped his Corona which drew everyone's attention. As everyone looked towards the Corona bottle, Conartist real smoothly switched the dice. Now with the trick-dice in his hands, KO, Con, and young George bet everyone who thought the dice would lose.

"Six-Dice!" yelled Con as he threw the dice up against the wall.

"Six-Dice."

Young Con tightly grips his hand around the dice and shakes them-as he threw the dice against the wall he screamed, "Scams, No-grams, I don't give a Damn!" as the dice hit the wall and landed on six.

As Con, KO, and George were picking up their winnings, someone burst through the door screaming that the cops were coming because of the Southbridge girls were on the rings floor fighting. After hearing cops and Southbridge girls, the three quickly exited the bathroom to a crowd of people standing in a circle. After breaking their way through the crowd, their young hearts dropped. Poundcake was on the floor crying while holding Alisha's lifeless body in her arms. Alisha had been stabbed multiple times in the chest.

CHAPTER 23

Emilly's Funeral

The Camden New Jersey Aquarium was the perfect place for young Con and Kelly's first date. Not wanting Kelly anywhere near the places, he roamed; Con decided to take her to New Jersey. After walking through the aquarium hand in hand, the two are now sitting in-front of the sharks tank talking about their likes dislikes, future and goals.

"So why do they call you Con?" asked Kelly with a curious look on her face.

"Who calls me Con? You know my name is Andrew," said Con with a devilish smile on his face.

"Boy stop playing, you know I've done my homework."

"So, what your checkin' up on me now?" asked Con with a smile on his face.

"Yup, because you never know these days."

"Well it's a long story, but one I'll be sure to tell you about," said young Conartist while ducking the question. As the two continued picking one another's brain, the closer they got.

While leaving out of Barbee's rich parents gated community, young Trickbaby sees a familiar looking Benz parked in the front of one of the many beautiful mansions.

"This can't be the mansion that everyone only heard of, but never believe existed. The mansion that's rumored to have one-million in a safe that's located in one of the closets, it can't be," thought young Trick.

While circling the block, Trick passes the mansion which has a sign on the door that reads: **"NEVER MIND THE DOG-BEWARE OF THE**

OWNER." In the white Barbee's tinted-out Acura, Trick is now parked in perfect view of the front entrance of the house. High off Percocet's-mixed with codeine syrup, has him mentally plotting on one of the deadliest capers thus far. Not thinking rationally, he has now blocked out trust, love and loyalty-for money over everything. Not focused and going against everything the Youngest-in-Charge were taught, Trick sits and waits.

After being parked for 30 minutes, the owners of the hearse "the ones that leaves people swimming the sharks" walks out of the mansions front door.

"We gather here today to celebrate the love that Mrs. Emilly brought to this world. Mrs. Emilly was surely one of God's children who would give you the shirt off of her back," said the Rev speaking to a packed church, "Mrs. Emilly wasn't just known in Wilmington but throughout the whole state of Delaware. She had 10 kids but her only biological child was Dula; the rest were adopted."

The packed pews were crying hysterically over the loss of sweet Mrs. Emilly and the ones who weren't crying were whispering or having negative thoughts about how Dula shitted on his mother. Some were wondering if he would show up for the funeral while others knew that if he hadn't showed up to save her, he wouldn't show up to see her leave.

Mrs. Emilly also has three sisters; however, one hasn't been seen in 30 years and has been reported missing. If she's still alive, her family and friends are in hope that Mrs. Emilly funeral will bring her out. As Mrs. Emilly's family and friends were still pouring into the church, Detective Lacy and undercover backups were parked across the street looking for any signs of Dula.

"Mrs. Emilly left us while doing God's work, she was in the middle of cooking for the homeless-on her birthday! The world is going to miss Mrs. Emilly," said the Rev as three women dressed in all-black entered the church.

The three women had on black hats and veils covering their faces, but the family knew just who they were-the sisters. Witnessing the sister walk up to the casket while holding hands caused the family to cry even louder. As the sisters sat down, the whispering started.

"That's the lost sister," whispered many.

Even the Rev noticed, "The Lord take'th and the Lord give'th," said the Rev speaking of the lost sister.

After an hour and a half of praising the Lord and Mrs. Emilly's life, the Rev informed the family that the burial would be at the Riverview Cemetery. As the pallbearers slowly carried the casket-followed by the three sisters, then the rest of the family, Detective Lacy focused in. After putting the casket into the hearse, the three sisters slowly walked to the families Limousine.

As the third sister went to enter the vehicle, Detective Lacy screamed, "Freeze!" as the rest of the undercover officers pulled their weapons as well.

The family is horrified as they looked towards the detective and the weapons that were being aimed at the sisters. The third sister not understanding the detective's orders continued to get into the Limo.

"If you take one more step," said the detective as the sister quickly reached in her pocketbook, "BOC! BOC! BOC! BOOM, BOOM, POW!" Were the sounds the family heard as the sister who took multiple gun shots fell between the open car door and the sidewalk.

As the detective aggressively kicked the pocketbook that held two 9 millimeters from out of the sister's hand, he pulled the veil from over her face and was staring in the eyes of a dead man-Dula.

CHAPTER 24

The Conclusion

<u>The Next Day</u>

"Ok check this out, Kim I sense that you are really stressed. How about we board a flight to Las Vegas for the weekend," said Marvin who's trying desperately to win Kim's heart.

Lately, Marvin has been persistent in trying to fuck Kim; even to the point that he now sometimes finds himself stalking her.

To Marvin, Kim has the best pussy he's ever had and to him, "It ain't tricking if you got it."

"You know what Marvin, I've been patient and kind to your feelings for too long and because you haven't been respecting my wishes, this is the space you put me in. I don't want to go to Las Vegas with you. I don't want your money and because you don't turn me on, I no longer want to have sex with you. And one more thing-I've met someone," said Kim frustrated that Marvin won't leave her alone.

Marvin is so hot that you can cook an egg on the top of his head; he's furious that Kim would talk to him that way.

"And just to let you know, I've put in for a transfer to another bank branch, so this will be my last week that I'll be working with you." Not wanting to hear anymore of Kim's disrespect, Marvin hung up the phone in her ear.

Now mad and thinking of ways to have Kim "missing," Marvin decides to take the day off. Still not believing that Marvin won't accept that she no-longer wants to be his high-price whore, she goes in the closet and gets the sex tape that she secretly made of her and young Con.

"The label of a SNITCH is a lifetime scar-you will always be in jail just minus the bars," sang young George who's singing along to Jay-z's lyrics that's coming out of the Audi S4 sound system. Because Porsha is coming home within the next day or two has George in a good mood and wanting to do something real special for her.

Now on his way to drop of some money to Alisha's mother who's been taking her loss hard, young George makes a pitstop to his crib to grab some CD's. After taking a shit, George is now in his bedroom looking for his Nas, Jadakiss, and Beanie-Seigal CD's. After only finding two of them, he silently cursing-out young Con for always touching his shit. On his way out the front door he sees a CD on the kitchen table and grabs it, thinking it was the CD he was looking for.

"You act like I put the toast to ya head and made you sale-We both came in this game blind as hell-I did a little better-had more clientele-Told you put away some bread-now you crying for bail-It was all good just a week ago."

"Damn!" screamed young George as his favorite Jay-Z CD continues to skip from being scratched. After taking the CD out, he puts the CD that he found on the kitchen table into the video monitor car system. What popped up on the monitor after he pushed "play" stopped his heart. As George watched young Con long-dick his mom from the back, tears continuously ran down his cheeks. Kim who was planning on giving the sex-tape to Marvin with the hopes that it would push him away, accidentally left it on the kitchen table.

"Skeez, why don't you, Woo and Lil' Ray got y'all's hair cut?" asked young Trick who's in the projects enjoying the warm summer evening.

"Because my mom said that we had to wait until she get her check," replied Skeez speaking of him and his two little brothers.

As Trick dug into his pocket to give Skeez money for their haircuts, he notices Skully eye-hustlin' from a distance.

"Dope-sick" and not knowing where to turn for a fix, Skully built-up the courage to confront Trick.

"Young Trick can I holla at you," said Skully scared of the response he may receive.

"What the Fuck this nigga want to talk to me about? This the same nigga that had his dick down my mom's throat," thought Trick but didn't show his anger.

"What it do Skully?"

"Trick, why are you so hard on me? I got nothing but love for you, but you treat me like I've done something to you."

"Skully, I ain't slow to nothing fast, so get to the point before I think you trying to run game on me," said Trick not wanting to hear any of Skully's pillow-talk Bullshit.

"Trick, I'm dope-sick, can I get a couple dollars so I can get a bag of dope?" Skully asked looking like a dressed-up trash can.

"You got your works?" asked young Trick speaking about the needle that Skully would use to shoot-up the heroin.

Happy that young Trick would be asking that question, Skully quickly answered, "Yes."

"Meet me on the back street next to my car," said Trick as he made his way towards the lab.

After 10 minutes of waiting next to Trick's black Chevy Impala, Skully sees young Trick walking around the corner with something in his hand. As the two got into the car, Trick handed Skully a small package of heroin.

"Thank you," said Skully as he is getting out of the car.

"Whole," said Trick as Skully looked back, "where are you going?" asked Trickbaby.

"I'm going to get this dope in me," answered Skully while looking confused.

"Nah Pimp, you gotta do that right here," said Trick with a serious look on his face.

"Trick, I got too much respect for you to be shooting heroin in front of you."

"Well, you must don't want to get high," said Trick.

Then with no hesitation, Skully pulled out his works and loaded the needle with the dope. After pulling-up his shirt sleeve, Skully injected the heroin. After three minutes of feeling warm inside, white foam started coming out of his mouth, as his chin hits his chest. Skully is now feeling the dope in his veins like Romello's pop from the movie Sugar Hill; with some of the pure heroin that he took from Yola, young Trick has rocked Skully to sleep.

"You Sad Ass Nigga, you won't be putting your dick in no-one else's mouth," said young Trick as he kicked the dead man out of his car and pulled off.

Through young KO receives a tremendous amount of love from his brothers from another mother, inside he still feels lonely from missing the only woman that ever loved him-his grandmother. His uncle AC, who has turned his back on him has KO feeling sad, hopeless and angry. Looking at the $500 money order he has in his hand; young Knock-out knows just who to direct his anger to his dad.

Dad, I write with no-intent to disrespect you; however, I ask that you will man-up and respect my feelings. You received a life-bit for killing a nigga over a piece of pussy that wasn't even yours. You left your only son for a piece of pussy. You left me at the tender age of three, who are you? I asked that because the truth is that, I really don't know you. The sad part is that I don't even feel comfortable calling you dad. All the money orders I've sent you in the past didn't have a letter attached, because I was suppressing my feelings. And by doing that causes me to hurt even more. I needed your support and you weren't there. Don't get it confused, I don't wear my emotions on my sleeves because the streets has raised an animal and I now run wit a pack of wolves. However, these streets don't love no-one and you left me to defend for myself. You know what, this is getting a little too emotional, but always remember that it's me against the world out here in these mean streets.
    KO

After putting the letter in the mailbox, young KO is in need of someone to help lift his spirits, so he's now on his way to pick up his man's young

Trickbaby.

After continuously calling young George and getting no answer, young Con drives through the projects looking for him. After seeing his car parked in front of the lab, Con quickly parks. Wanting to talk to young George about an up and coming caper, young Con walks into the lab while leaving the backdoor unlocked. Once entering the living room, Con sees George sitting in the chair and holding a .40 Cal in his lap.

Realizing something is wrong, young Con cautiously asks George, "What was going on?"

"Murder," said George as he pushed play on the portable DVD player.

As Con watched himself fuck Kim from the back, George raises the .40 Cal to Con's head and asked, "Why?" Shocked, regretful and feeling guilty, young Con is lost for words.

"You betrayed me," said George as a single tear rolled down his cheek.

"Put the gun down George, I'm sorry," said Con while looking George straight in his eyes.

Not accepting Con's sorrows, George wraps his finger around the trigger.

"Hold George! It's me, your childhood friend. We were birthed in the same sandbox, shared park lunches and even slept on each other's couches," pleaded young Con as his eyes started to fill with tears.

Con was hurting, but not so much for the act itself, but for the hurt and pain he sees in his best friends eyes.

"There go their cars right there," said the female as she directed the farmer and cigarette guru Akil to park.

"Motha fucka, you violated me! You know its death before dishonor!"

George yelled as his hand began to shake, but gun still aimed at Con's head.

"George, I'm not trying to make any excuses, I was wrong. However, she applied so much pressure on me that I fell victim. Listen Main-man, I tried many times to dodge her aggressive behavior, but she was so persuasive and seductive that I lost the battle," said Con hoping the truth shall set him free.

As the female knocked on the door she got no answer but heard two familiar voices which seemed to be arguing. Not expecting the door to be unlocked, the female turned the knob and walked in.

After making it to the living room-Porsha screamed, "NOOOOO!"

As George yelled, "Nigga you gotta know when to roll and when to fold!" BOC! BOC!

As young Trickbaby walked into the house he heard his mom Shaneequa in her bedroom crying hysterically. Not wasting any time, Trick quickly ran up the steps and softly knocked on her bedroom door.

After not receiving an answer, Trick took it upon himself to walk in. Shaneequa who is still crying, is lying on her bed in a fetal position. Seeing this, young Trick with rapid speed, made it to her bedside.

He put his arms around her then asked, "What was wrong?"

"They found Skully on the back-street dead," answered Shaneequa as her sobs became louder.

Young Trick thought it was something more serious that had his mom crying a river, but after finding out her reasons, calmed his nerves.

After 15 minutes of comforting her, Shaneequa has yet to calm down which has Trick wondering why. He knows that Shaneequa and Skully's friendship go way back, but to him she's going overboard with it and he doesn't know why.

After another five minutes of hugging and wiping her tears, Shaneequa finally calmed down.

"Baby, can you please make me some hot tea?" asked Shaneequa as she dampened her eyes with a washcloth. As Trick opened the bedroom door to go make the tea, she called his name.

As young Trick turned to look back Shaneequa said, "That was your father."

Not completely understanding what she meant, Trick passive-aggressively asked, "What?"

"Skully was your father," said Shaneequa as the tears started up again.

After quickly processing what his mom just told him, young Trick slammed the door behind him and went to his room. Now filled with guilt, shame and unbearable pain, Trick sits on his bed as tears rolls down his cheeks. After all these years of picturing Skully's dick in the back of Shaneequa's throat brought on feelings that couldn't be explained. If only Trick would have known that Skully was his father, his life would have probably turned out differently, even including his name-Trickbaby. To medicate the pain, Trick ate eight Percocet-thirties and drank a bottle of codeine syrup like it was water.

"Who is it?" asked Shaneequa as she opens the front door.

"Where's Trick?" asked KO as Shaneequa pointed towards the steps.

While running up the steps KO yells out Tricks name but gets no answer.

After opening the bedroom door, young KO sees Trick's body stretched out on the floor with white foam coming out of his mouth. Like-father, like-son, Trickbaby has overdosed. Seeing the Percocet bottle lying next to Trick's body, KO immediately pulls out his phone and calls the ambulance. As young Trick lifeless body lays on the floor, his soul is speaking with the All Mighty God and asking for just one more chance.

"I submit and wish to take off to new horizons, climax to higher heights to an unorthodox magnitude or board a never-ending flight. Enter a totally different timeline, realm, or dimension. I yearn to experience Your unlimited love; You now have my undivided attention. I'm asking for Your divine Heavenly Blessings exceedingly beyond measure. Each and every one of them I promise to cherish like treasure. Please enlighten and surround me with supernatural unearthly works. The All Powerful and All Majestic, the remainder of my life, I'll put You first. Every second of every day, I'll worship You, my life will be a living prayer. It doesn't matter which way I turn; Your presence will always be there. I'm in awe by Your reassurance, in me, Your Spirit is deeply rooted, please embrace me and show me what the truth is. Pull the veil from my eyes, Your reflection in my reality is crystal clear. I seek You with pure diligence and will keep my head to the clouds. I see Your Face in Your creation; I hear Your Voice in every sound. I anticipate Your descent in the third part of every night. Please dissipate and consume my darkness with Your illuminating light. I'll be grateful for providing for me my every need. For the wise, I'll be a sign for those in doubt to believe. SAVE ME!"

ABOUT THE AUTHOR

Mr. Andrew Raymere Hansley known to most as Ray was born in Wilmington Delaware. He was raised in the Southbridge and the 2-6 Projects by a single parent but with the help of his grandmother. As a kid he played all sports, with football and boxing being his favorites. He was the oldest of five, Ms. Julianna Hansley had four boys and one girl. Mr. Hansley's father was in jail, so he turnt to the streets to find that fatherly love. After realizing his mother couldn't give him the finer things in life; he made a decision to get it how he lived.

Ray childhood friends was just as hungry as he was. So along with Mr. Hansley, they started collecting cans, pumping gas, carrying groceries-and cutting grass, as well. Because that wasn't enough for Mr. Hansley he also started stealing. By the age of 12 Ray had a full fledge gambling habit. He shot dice, played cards, shot pool, and bowled-all for the love of the hustle. Ray's mothers' side of the family lived in one project and his father lived another; so, he was back and forth while picking up game with every step he took. The thorough old heads from both neighborhoods loved him and was always dropping a jewel on him.

By the age of 13 and 14 the illusion that the game brings had already settled in his young mind, because now the latest Jordon, gun, and gold chain was all he lived for.

At the age 15, Ray purchased his first car, not even two months later he got busted with 500 grams of powder cocaine. Because he was just juvie, they sentenced him to a year. After being released, wasting no time at all, he jumped right back in the mix.

At the age 18 Ray got knocked off again with 280 grams of crack in which he was sentenced to 15 years. While doing his bit, he received his GED high school diploma and some college credits in Criminal Justice and Psychology. While in the belly of the beast Ray even ran a couple of therapeutic communities. After doing ten years he was given the opportunity to make parole. Two weeks later he was back on the bricks—only this time with a different mindset.

The Struggle Live's On!

The Youngest-in-Charge – Part 2

Coming Soon!

I didn't sell my soul to the Devil; I bought his from him...

"Young George, I'm telling you this because I love you. Never get so comfortable with pain that you forget happiness is still an option. Stop giving 100% to people who only gives 50%. Main-man, happiness comes from within, never assign anyone else that much power over your life. It's time to take care of you-and put your own needs first. George, you gotta eliminate what don't help you get money-evolve. It don't have to make since, it just have to make you money..." said One of the triplets.

"I rather be carried by six than to be judged by 12," said KO.

"Baby I miss us..." said Poundcake.

"If lovin' you was a crime, I'll do time for you..." replied Kim.

"As long as you're taking care of business with my heart, you'll never have to worry about my love. Love is so blind that it feels right even when it's wrong. See it's something about a hood-nigga's swag that attracts pretty suburban queens. How are you going to love me, when you don't even love yourself? Love is a verb, it's what you do. It's an action that always speaks louder than words. You think you hurt me with this disgusting move, well, it's nothing compared to what you have done to yourself," said Kelly.

I'm not trying to hear that Bull-shit, tell me something I ain't heard before."

"Young Con, you are somebody, you mean something, you matter. You're not asking for too much, you're just asking the wrong person."

"Naw, Fuck that, I get it how I live, I shine different from them crabs; when a wave comes, you gotta flow wit-it. If you can't feel good-you gotta look good," said young Conartist.

It's FINSHED!

RAY & RICK

This young entrepreneur is not just one of Southbridge's Finest, He's also my son; A college graduate who still has his innocence. This kid inspires many. He came from the same poverty stricken neighborhood that most fell victim to the illusion that the streets bring. However, this handsome young fella didn't allow the streets to swallow him whole. Although he has been around and seen all the things the mean streets can bring.

Shaquille Rayon Davis is the CEO/Owner of the clothing line **"Never Look Back"** which offers Sweat Suits, Shirts, Hats, Pants, ECT. Go to his Instagram page to see much more @nvrlookbackclothing.

Another one of South-Bridges finest used his intelligence to put a clothing business together that's growing every-day. When at his lowest, he put his bag on his shoulders and carried his own weight. This loyal Lil homie of mines has inspired many. He loves his projects and his projects love's him back.

Mr. Thomas Jackson better known as "Gash the Great," is the CEO and Owner of **Carry My Own Weight Clothing Line** that offers hats, shirts, pants, sweatsuits, etc.

For more information call 302-691-5599

Web: www.CarryMyOwnWeight.Com

Facebook--Carry My Own Weight.